*A*
*CANDLELIGHT REGENCY SPECIAL*

# CANDLELIGHT REGENCIES

# LOVE'S FOLLY

## Nina Pykare

### A CANDLELIGHT REGENCY SPECIAL

Published by
Dell Publishing Co., Inc.
1 Dag Hammarskjold Plaza
New York, New York 10017

Dell ® TM 681510, Dell Publishing Co., Inc.

ISBN: 0-440-14959-2

Printed in the United States of America

First printing—October 1980

For
my mother,
who taught me
the value of love.

And
my father,
who showed me
what a man could be.

# LOVE'S FOLLY

# CHAPTER 1

The road that wound from the heart of Essex into London was generously warmed by the bright spring sun. Near the edge of the road two aged grooms slowly repaired a loose wagon wheel on a fashionable carriage, pausing now and then to wipe the sweat from their brows. The occupants of the carriage—a vivacious young woman of nineteen, a quiet, slightly older one, and a silent maidservant—had apparently found the heat of the carriage intolerable and had spread a mantle in the shade of a tree some distance away. From this position they watched the grooms at work.

"They are so terribly slow," cried the younger woman, her hands adjusting the bonnet that topped her blond curls. "I want to get to London today. I've so much to do before the Victory Celebration."

"Emily, my dear," said the older one. "Bond Street will not vanish overnight. Surely you can do your shopping another day."

"Yes, yes, Sarah. I know that. But I've waited so long. I yearn for the city."

Sarah Parker shook her head and sighed. Young Emily Penthorne was a good girl, but a little high-spirited. Being her companion was a somewhat difficult task.

Emily smiled the sweet smile of a girl who has always had her way. "Dear Sarah, you are so patient with me. I am most fortunate to have you for a cousin. I know I am impatient. It's just . . ."

Sarah smiled fondly. Emily was a lovable girl. After all, who could blame her for being a little wild when she had lost her mother so young?

"It's just that we've been in Essex so long," continued Emily, "that I can't wait to get back to the city. I had so much fun during my first season." She did not let her face reflect that other reason that she had carried secretly in her heart since last year. It would not do for Sarah to know that.

"You must not expect the young men to be quite so attentive this year," cautioned Sarah. "There will be other girls just come out."

Emily smiled the mischievous smile of a child.

"But I am very pretty, am I not, Sarah? Surely some young man will want to marry me." She made herself say the words, but she knew in her heart that she would never marry. Not unless she could find the dark stranger that she had seen at Lady Cholmondoley's that night. She had noticed him regarding her with dark piercing eyes and she had colored and lowered her gaze. Then, when she looked again, he was gone, vanished. She had not seen him again, though she had looked and looked.

A flicker of pain crossed Sarah's face as Emily spoke of marriage, but her charge was too lost in her own thoughts to notice it. "I'm sure there will be men eager to offer for you," Sarah replied. "But you must be careful. Everyone knows the extent of your inheritance. You must not be surprised to find that it is your portion rather than your person that excites a man's interest."

Emily wrinkled her small nose. "Oh, don't be such a serious puss, Sarah. I just want to have some fun." That was to be her excuse for not accepting any offers of marriage if they were made her. It seemed rather shallow, but how could she say that she had formed a partiality for a stranger she had only glimpsed once? And a strong partiality it was, too.

Sarah smiled. "Fun is fine in its place—*if* you remember that marriage is a lifetime concern, not to be taken lightly."

Emily smiled ruefully. "Dear Sarah, I know. But it has been deadly dull in Essex." She shook her head. "I wonder that I could have stood it for so long."

Sarah patted her charge's small gloved hand. "It is only since your season that you have found the country dull. Before that you much enjoyed life in Essex."

Emily's blue eyes danced. "I was a child then, enjoying childish things. Now I am a woman."

Sarah merely nodded. It was not her place to tell her charge that she had a great deal more growing to do before she reached womanhood.

Suddenly Emily got to her feet, her hands automatically smoothing down her gown of pale blue muslin and its matching pelisse. "Oh, Sarah, it was so grand last year. My coming out and all the balls. The theater and Vauxhall. I simply cannot wait."

"Emily, you must be patient, dear. You have given no thought to your Uncle Cyril. He is getting along in years. Perhaps he will prefer to lead a quiet life."

Emily turned a woeful face to her cousin. "Oh dear, Sarah, please don't say so!" Then her expression cleared. "Besides, Uncle Cyril is such a dear. I'm sure he will listen to me." She must be out in society, she thought, or she would never find *him*, that dark stranger from the ball.

Sarah nodded. They had not been long in Lon-

don for Emily's first season when it had become
abundantly clear that the girl could wrap her old
uncle around her little finger. Fortunately Sarah
had been able to exercise some subtle control so
Emily had not run amuck. But this year Sarah was
not so sure she could manage. Emily was older
now and more headstrong. Probably the adulation
of the beaus had given her a sense of power.

"I must walk about a little, Sarah. Just a little.
You sit still now."

Sarah nodded. In the country there was no harm
in Emily's walking about alone.

As she walked slowly toward the carriage,
Emily paused now and then to observe a bright
wildflower or a newly budding leaf. She did love
the country. There was no doubt about that. Surely this spring had been as beautiful as any. But
somehow all the old things—the blooming hedge-
rows, the fields of daffodils, the bright blue sky,
the green grass—none of these were sufficient anymore. Something was missing.

There was inside her a deep and undefinable
yearning—a yearning for something nameless.
When she had tried to talk to Sarah about it, her
cousin had merely smiled and said, "You are growing up. This yearning is for a partner with whom
to share your life."

And Emily had said no more. She was quite determined she would share her life with no man
but that dark stranger.

13

Sometimes it had frightened her to think of entrusting her life to a stranger. How could she live with someone she knew nothing of? Leg-shackled, Cousin Percy called it. But now she saw. If the man were that stranger, why, she would be willing. At least she had one advantage in her search for him, she thought as she stooped to admire a violet. Uncle Cyril was an old dear. He would never insist that she marry any *particular* man.

The sound of hooves caused her to raise her head. Another carriage was approaching. She paused beside a tree, the violet in her hand, half-conscious that she made a pretty picture there in the sunlight.

The carriage passed by at a comfortable clip. Emily's hand went to her mouth in surprise. The man whose face was framed by the carriage window, the man whose dark eyes met and held hers, was the stranger of the ball! She knew it was ill-conceived to stare at a man like that. She was not at all in the habit of quizzing strangers. But to have him appear like that—just when she was thinking of him—had taken her by surprise.

As his carriage rattled on, Emily sank to the grass. How well she remembered him—the darkly handsome face, the unruly black hair, and the black, piercing eyes that seemed able to probe her very soul. Color flooded her cheeks at the thought of his eyes meeting hers. Had he remembered her? she wondered. And did he think she made a pretty picture standing there? She hoped so. Suddenly her need to reach London was even stronger. *He* was going to be there!

She moved on toward the carriage. "How soon?" she asked the grooms, her voice clearly indicating her anxiety to be on her way.

" 'Tis sorry I am, miss, but such things takes time."

"I know, Hodges." Emily's voice was contrite. "It's just that I'm so anxious."

"I know, miss. We'll be having this done soon now. Don't you be worrying none."

Emily nodded at this and turned back toward her cousin. She would talk to Sarah, perhaps that way she could still the beating of her heart. Strange that just seeing the man should affect her so.

She made bright conversation with Sarah, but the picture of the stranger persisted in her mind. She must find him. She must go everywhere until he appeared.

Eventually the mended carriage moved on toward the city and Emily's excitement grew. "Oh, Sarah," she cried as they entered London. "I do love the city. There's so much happening. Time passes so quickly here."

"I much prefer the peace of the country myself," Sarah replied calmly. "But I believe I can understand your feeling."

"It's a whole different world," said Emily. "Not

like Essex at all. Look, Sarah. There's the same little old lady that sold tea and hot buns last year."

"Yes, I see her."

"And there goes a butcher's boy with a great side of beef. See how the shopgirls eye him. Ugh. That beef doesn't look very tasty."

Sarah smiled. "Of course it doesn't. But I'm sure Cook could make a good meal of it."

"Cook can do wonders," agreed Emily. "But I like best her apple tarts." She clapped her gloved hands together merrily. "Look, there's a girl selling posies. How pretty they are."

"Bakin' or boilin' apples," came the cry from a buxom woman whose red cheeks shone from the heat of the charcoal stove beside her barrow. As Emily watched, a dapper gentleman stepped up and purchased two apples, then returned to a near-by carriage where he handed one to a lady who smiled at him sweetly.

A strange twinge occurred inside Emily's breast. Would she smile thus someday at the man who was to be her husband? Would she even find the stranger?

Down one side of the street came a peddler. Loaded with brooms, brushes, sieves, bowls, and other items, he was a curious sight. But his face, as he proclaimed his wares, wore a happy smile.

"Lavender. Buy my lavender," cried a child nearby. Emily turned to look. The girl could not have been more than twelve.

"Sarah, couldn't we buy a bunch? Just one?"

"I'm sure your uncle will have made adequate provision for the linen presses in St. James's Square," said Sarah with a smile. "But if you want some for yourself, I see no harm in it."

"Good."

The driver of the carriage was soon directed to follow the child and Emily made her purchase, feeling as much joy at the smile on the child's face as at the sweet scent of the lavender in her hands.

As the carriage moved on again Emily noticed a man carrying a pole across his shoulders from which were suspended several dead rabbits. "Look, Sarah," she cried. "There goes a higgler. How furious Uncle Cyril would be to see him. He must have gotten those rabbits from poachers."

Sarah sighed. "I wonder at the risks men take. The penalty for poaching is quite severe. I believe it may mean transportation."

Emily shivered. "How dreadful! But, oh, look! There are several fashionable ladies."

Sarah, looking in the indicated direction, frowned. "Emily, my dear, pray do me a favor and do not speak of such ladies."

"Whyever not?" asked her charge, who was eagerly cataloging every item of the ladies' apparel.

"Because they are not ladies," said Sarah.

"But they are dressed so fine!"

"They are incognitas," replied Sarah with a deeper frown. "Women who make their fortunes by selling themselves."

"They look very happy," observed Emily.

"Emily!"

She turned bright blue eyes on her cousin. "What is it, Sarah?"

"You must not say such outlandish things." Sarah plucked nervously at her gloves. "I know that you mean nothing by it, but others would not. The ladies of the *ton* would be deeply shocked."

Emily frowned. "I only stated what I observed. They *do* look happy."

"Looks can be deceiving."

Emily's eyes sparkled with sudden merriment. "Dear Sarah, do not grow so serious. I am not contemplating such a course of life."

"I should hope not!"

Emily patted her cousin's hand. "Sarah, dear, you still can't tell when I'm funning you."

Sarah smiled rather weakly. "Emily, Emily. The *ton* does not appreciate this kind of funning. When you are in society, you must be more careful!"

"Yes, Sarah, I shall." Emily made the promise, but she thought privately that dear as she was, Cousin Sarah was a little stick-in-the-muddish. However, Emily added to herself quite truthfully, a girl couldn't ask for a nicer companion than Sarah. It was a terrible shame that she had been left penniless as she had when her parents died.

It had been fortunate for Sarah that Emily needed a companion at the time; but it had been equally fortunate for Emily to get Sarah. On occasion her high spirits had been dampened by Sarah's cautions. But last year, during her first season when they had come to the city, Emily had fully realized what a gem she had in Sarah. A diamond of the first water, as Cousin Percy would say, though he used the phrase in reference to the physical rather than spiritual beauty that Sarah possessed.

By now the character of the passersby had changed. As they approached St. James's Square the streets grew less crowded with tradespeople. Emily began to wiggle around on the seat like an eager child, until, feeling Sarah's gentle eyes upon her, she managed to compose herself.

There was something about the city that she found most exciting. It was so lively and interesting—with so much going on. She could hardly wait to be part of it again. And now she had a chance to find *him!*

The coach moved into St. James's Square and Emily craned her neck to look out the window at the familiar houses. "I shall be so glad to see Uncle," she said. "It seems just ages."

Sarah nodded. "I hope you find your uncle in good health."

"I'm sure he will be," returned Emily eagerly. "Oh, I am so excited."

As the carriage drew up to the door, she could

contain herself no longer and burst from it. Half-running, half-walking, she hurried to the door. Behind her in the carriage Sarah heaved a sigh. This season would be much more difficult than the last. She felt it in her bones.

# CHAPTER 2

"Miss Emily!" Parks greeted her with obvious enjoyment.

"Oh, Parks!" Emily almost hugged the corpulent butler but, remembering in time that she was no longer a schoolroom miss, she contented herself with giving him a bright smile.

"His lordship is waiting for you in his rooms. His gout is giving him trouble again. He'll be happy to see you, so he will."

"I'll go right to him. Miss Sarah is coming with our boxes. Do help her."

"Yes, miss. Of course."

Emily hurried up the stairs toward her uncle's rooms. She did not like to think of anyone she cared for being sick. An extremely healthy person herself, she found the thought of sickness very frightening. Then, too, it wakened bad memories of the time when her parents had sickened and died.

She burst into her uncle's rooms. "Uncle Cyril! Parks said you are ill!"

The white-haired man in the great chair before the fire smiled at her fondly. "Easy, child," he said, raising a detaining hand. "It's just the gout."

"Oh, Uncle, I'm so sorry." Emily threw herself to the floor beside the chair and enveloped her uncle in a tender hug.

His lordship managed to extricate himself from her embrace. "Emily, my dear. You are looking prettier than ever."

"Yes, Uncle, I know. Isn't it grand?"

Lord Hamston laughed heartily. "What a brazen minx you are, Emily."

"But Uncle," Emily said, turning innocent blue eyes to him. "Mama always said the truth was best. And I *am* pretty." She and the old man often played this game. It seemed to amuse him and she did not mind.

His lordship smiled. "You're right enough about that," he said with a chuckle. "But the young gentlemen would not be pleased to hear you say so. They much prefer to originate the words of praise."

"Of course, Uncle. I shall remember."

"Please do, young lady. Now, pull up a chair here. We must have a talk."

"Yes, Uncle."

As she pulled the chair closer, Emily noticed that the past year had left its marks on her uncle. His round face, always jovial when he was speaking, looked careworn in repose. She sighed. There was really no way to avoid the realization that her uncle was aging.

"My dear Emily." Lord Hamston cleared his throat before he continued. "I am very pleased to see you in London."

"And I am pleased to see *you*, Uncle." Emily wondered what it was he wanted to speak to her about. Surely it couldn't be this.

Lord Hamston looked at her again. "Well, my dear. It's like this. I'm an old man, ill and crochety." He raised a hand to silence her protests. "I can no longer fulfill my duties as your guardian."

Emily was bewildered. "What does this mean?" she asked in a subdued tone. Surely he would not send her back to the country. He couldn't—not now when she had waited so long, not now when she had a chance to find *him*. She looked at her uncle with anxious eyes.

"I am going to Bath," he continued, "to take the waters there. I shall leave early in the morning. I have only just waited so that I could see you. I have given over my duties to my nephew, Viscount Dunstan, who has just returned from fighting Napoleon."

Emily heaved a sigh of relief. Her visit to the city was safe.

"I hope you understand, my dear." He patted her hand.

"Of course, Uncle. You're so kind to me. Don't bother yourself about it. I shall miss you, though."

Lord Hamston sighed. "You're a good child, my dear. I shall miss you, too. But I shall return before the cold sets in. These old bones need a snug place then. Dunstan will be back before dinner. You can talk to him then. In the meantime I believe I shall have to take a nap."

"Of course, Uncle." Emily smiled. "Perhaps Sarah and I will go to Bond Street. I haven't been to the shops for so long."

Her uncle waved a tired hand. "Do as you please, my dear. Though I should think your bones would be worn out with all that jostling."

Emily got to her feet. "Have a nice nap, Uncle. I'll see you at dinner."

She dropped a kiss on his forehead and then left the room. Perhaps they would see *him* on Bond Street, she thought, her heart beginning to pound. After all, he had been on his way to London.

"Parks! Oh, Parks!" she cried as she hurried down the stairs. "Tell my driver to stay put. Sarah and I are going shopping directly our things are unloaded."

As Emily reached her, Sarah frowned and remonstrated. "Perhaps you had better wait and consult with your new guardian," she said.

"I see that you have heard the news," cried Emily. "But, dear Sarah, don't be a wet blanket. I've been waiting the whole of the winter for this day."

"It would hardly hurt you to wait one more day," Sarah observed dryly.

"I know, I know. But Uncle is going to take a nap. And really, Sarah, I feel that if I do not get to the shops immediately, I shall burst."

To this Sarah had no reply, and as Emily was already mounting the steps to the carriage, she had little recourse but to follow.

As they moved from shop to shop, Emily grew increasingly merry. "Oh, Sarah, do look at this darling little hat. I simply must have it."

The hat in question was by no means little, being what is called a poke bonnet and having a brim that greatly resembled the bottom of a shovel. On top of it danced a profusion of artificial daisies.

Despite all Sarah's protests the hat was purchased and added to the growing pile of bundles and boxes in the carriage.

"Oh, oh, Sarah, do look at this material. Isn't this pattern most charming?"

25

Several of the purchases caused Sarah to frown, especially the ordering of one gown. "What will the viscount say to a gown like that?" she asked, only to be met by a merry laugh.

"Dear Sarah, he will not concern himself with my clothes. Uncle never has. And the money is mine to spend as I will. You know I have several quarters' allowance."

This fact was incontrovertible and effectively silenced Sarah, but Emily could tell from her companion's expression that she was not at all happy about the shopping expedition. "There, Sarah," she said as they left the last shop in a row of several, "I have expended some of my energy and now I can wait patiently for another day. Shall we go home?"

"Yes, let us indeed."

The dryness of her companion's tone caused Emily to wrinkle her nose. No one seemed to understand. Life was exciting! There was so much to do. How could anyone bear to just sit, as Uncle Cyril did, with his gouty leg stretched out on a stool before him, and wait for visitors? Did no one remember how exciting it was to be young— with the world waiting before one?

Looking at Sarah's tired face, Emily felt a wave of contrition. "Oh, Sarah, I am sorry. I did not think about your being fatigued from the journey. Please forgive me."

Sarah shook her head. "I am a little tired, but

it is nothing. I am concerned, however, about your shopping. It is my place to restrain you, and I did not."

"Dear Sarah, you worry far too much. I have plenty of money. Why shouldn't I spend it?"

Sarah shook her head. "Men are not all like your Uncle Cyril. Your new guardian may be much stricter with you."

"Do you know anything about him?" asked Emily. "Do you know if he's a tyrant?"

"Emily! I did not use that word."

"Well, it's what you meant. I'm telling you now, Sarah, I won't stand for it. I simply won't. No man's going to treat me like a child!"

"Emily, my dear, calm yourself. I know very little of Viscount Dunstan. If I remember correctly, he distinguished himself in the fighting. He was wounded, I believe. But as to the rest of his character, I'm afraid I know nothing."

"Well, Sarah, we shall know about him soon enough. But let's not borrow trouble, as Papa used to say. I shall meet with the viscount before dinner. Probably he is quite a pleasant man."

Sarah sighed. "I hope so—for both our sakes."

By this time the carriage had reached the house on St. James's Square and they both gathered up some bundles. "Send some footmen," Emily told Parks. "There are more packages in the carriage. Many more."

"Yes, miss. Right away."

They had barely gotten all the packages up to Emily's room, where Rose had just finished unpacking their trunks, when a knock sounded on the door. Sarah opened it.

"His lordship, the viscount, wishes to see Miss Penthorne in the library," announced a footman.

Emily scowled. "Oh, botheration. I did so want to unpack my things. Tell him I'll be along in a little while." She turned back to the cashmere she was unpacking, but to her surprise there came the sound of the footman clearing his throat. She looked at him. "Yes, what is it?"

The footman was very young, a stripling almost, and he looked at her sheepishly before he managed to get the words out. "If you please, miss . . . That is . . . Well, miss, his lordship, the viscount, now . . . he ain't the sort as takes kindly to waiting. I guess it's from him having commanded and all. But miss, well, when he says jump, why, folks is wise to jump."

Obviously a little dismayed by his own temerity, the youth colored and dropped his eyes.

Emily felt herself bristling up. She did not intend to let any arrogant man run her life. Still, it might be wiser to go right away. "Thank you . . ." She looked at him questioningly.

"Jeffers, miss."

"Thank you, Jeffers. Please tell his lordship I shall be down right away."

"Yes, miss."

Emily took off her bonnet and tossed it onto the bed. "I suppose I may as well see what the man wants."

Sarah raised a warning eyebrow. "You better not go with your hackles up," she warned. "Jeffers is right. If the viscount is used to command, he may not take kindly to having a chit of a girl give him hard words."

"Sarah! Whose side are you on?"

"Your side, my dear. You know it. I am just asking you to be sensible. This man has power over you. That's a fact you would do well to recognize."

Emily shrugged. "We'll see." She cast a quick look in the mirror and hurried toward the door. "Mustn't keep Lord High-in-the-instep waiting."

She was gone before Sarah could remonstrate.

After all, Emily told herself, this guardian was a man. She would just smile at him sweetly and he would see things her way. Papa and Uncle Cyril always had.

She paused momentarily before the library door and put a bright smile on her face. Then she pushed it open and entered.

The man who stood with his back to her was examining a book on one of the shelves. His shoulders were quite broad, she noted absently; even a coat that was a little threadbare could not hide that. His buckskins looked as though they had had hard wear too. He was rather tall and lean, and dark unruly curls overlapped the back of his cravat and the collar of his coat.

"Parks said you wish to speak to me, mil—"

The word died in her throat as the man turned and she beheld—the stranger! It was him! But it couldn't be. Emily raised a shaking hand to her cheek.

The stranger looked somewhat surprised, too, but he recovered more quickly. "Please sit down, Miss Penthorne. We have several matters to discuss."

"Yes, milord." As if in a daze, Emily took the chair he indicated.

He drew up another beside her. "I suppose Uncle Cyril has told you that he passed your guardianship to me."

Emily nodded.

"It is not a task that I undertake willingly," he continued. "But Uncle is ailing and I hope to spare him the trouble and aggravation."

In spite of her bemused state, this roused Emily. "I have caused Uncle no trouble or aggravation," she felt compelled to reply.

The viscount smiled grimly. "I'm afraid my uncle sees the case somewhat differently," he began.

"But I have never—" Emily protested.

"Let us disregard the past," interrupted the viscount. "I know what Uncle told me. He finds the care of a girl like yourself trying."

30

"I am not a girl," cried Emily, now thoroughly incensed. "I am a woman! And I am not trying!" How could she have been so mistaken about this man? To think that she had spent months mooning over his memory. The thought made her even angrier.

Dunstan shook his head. "You may protest all you please. I saw you earlier today."

"What do you mean?" Emily asked indignantly, although she was afraid she knew the answer already.

"It is ill-advised for young women"—he said the word mockingly—"to be quizzing strange men by the roadside."

"But—" Emily could find no words to exonerate herself. The truth was her only defense, but she certainly could not tell this tyrant, this arrogant lord, that she had stared so because she had spent the winter dreaming of him. How that would amuse him.

"There's—there's nothing wrong with quizzing someone," she asserted. "The ladies of the *ton* do it constantly."

He sighed in exasperation. "In London perhaps. At the theater or the opera. But not on the road. Such conduct is not only ill-advised, it is dangerous. I forbid you to behave in this fashion again."

"Forbid!" Emily half rose from her chair in indignation, but he merely nodded as though she had agreed with him.

"And now, I understand that you went shopping today."

"Yes, I did. But it was *my* money."

The viscount's face took on a pained expression. "I am quite aware of that. That is not the issue here."

"Then what is?" Emily was growing more and more truculent. How dared he treat her in this abominable fashion!

"The issue is that as your guardian it is my duty to oversee your purchases. Shall we go upstairs and look them over?"

This time Emily rose to her feet. "You cannot mean it!" She was very angry now. It was extremely irritating to be treated like this—like a stupid little girl.

"*Au contraire,*" said his lordship. "I *do* mean it. I intend to see every item you have purchased and to ascertain whether or not it is suitable for my ward."

"I—I am not a child," sputtered Emily, glaring at him fiercely.

"Then I suggest you stop acting like one. One of the marks of maturity is having the sense to accept the inevitable."

As he then rose and moved toward the stairs, there was little for Emily to do but follow. It was quite unbelievable, she told herself. The man she had spent the winter dreaming about had turned out to be the world's greatest tyrant. To think that she had once believed herself to have formed a partiality for this man! To think that she had once wished for the chance to be leg-shackled to him for life!

## CHAPTER 3

The viscount went directly to her room and Emily followed, fuming. As the door opened, Sarah looked up from beside the bed where, knowing that her charge would wish to examine every purchase, she had been laying them out. "Emily!" she exclaimed.

"Sarah, this is Viscount Dunstan. He insists on seeing what we have bought." Emily's rage was barely under control.

"Your lordship," said Sarah. "I am Miss Penthorne's companion, Sarah Parker."

"So my uncle told me," said Dunstan. "I'm sure you'll be pleased to have some help taming our wild one here."

35

Emily bridled further. What a condescending way to speak of her.

"Emily is not wild," said Sarah evenly. "She is perhaps a little thoughtless at times—as we all are. But she will learn."

That ought to show him, thought Emily, but he merely smiled as though placating a child and looked around the room for a chair. He chose one and settled himself comfortably, stretching his long legs in riding buckskins out before him. "Now let me see what you have bought."

Behind his back Emily made a face, but Sarah ignored it and motioned her toward the bed.

And so every item from a pair of gloves to a shawl had to be examined by his lordship.

"Let me see that bonnet on you," he said when Emily showed him the bonnet she had found so delightful. Obediently she put it on.

The viscount frowned. It considerably marred his good looks, she thought grimly as she stood before him waiting. Angry as she was at such terrible treatment, there was no denying that Dunstan was a prime article. Any woman could see that. No wonder he had been so often in her thoughts. Of course, she told herself, that had only been before she knew anything of his character.

The viscount eyed her carefully, his head tilted to one side. "That bonnet should go back," he said finally.

"But why?" In her anger and humiliation Emily

found herself close to tears. No man had ever regulated her purchase of wearing apparel. Papa had left that task to Mama, and when Uncle Cyril had become her guardian, he had left it to Sarah.

"The bonnet is too old for you," he said soberly. "It's too large for the slenderness of your neck. And those bobbing artificial daisies are atrocious."

"I like it," she retorted stubbornly, swallowing over the lump in her throat. "The milliner assured me it's all the fashion."

The viscount shrugged. "That may well be. The point is this—the bonnet does not become you. Send it back."

"Yes, milord," interjected Sarah, giving Emily a warning look. "We'll do so immediately."

Emily removed the maligned bonnet and was about to throw it rather violently onto the bed when Sarah rescued it by almost snatching it from her hands.

The several cashmeres she had bought passed his lordship's appraisal, though, and when he hesitated over her favorite—the one with the deep blue threads in the border—Emily held her breath. She let it out with a sigh of relief when he finally nodded.

It was demeaning, she thought as she folded the shawl and turned to the other items, to be treated like this. He acted as though she were a child—and one without much understanding at that.

The viscount approved her dozen pair of white

kid gloves for evening wear, her six pair of lemon,
stone, and lilac for walking, and her York tan ones
for riding. He approved her mantle of gray cloth
with a hood and front ties, lined in blue, her satin
slippers in various shades; her kid half-boots for
walking; her pagoda-shaped parasol with the
telescopic steel stick; her two dozen handkerchiefs
edged in lace; her reticule of black velvet and
those to match her gowns; her beehive bonnet of
plaited straw—without artificial flowers. As he approved each item, Emily felt her tension lessening.
Perhaps they would be able to deal together after
all.

Finally she and Sarah stopped; nothing remained except one small pile of nightwear and
underclothing. "I presume you also ordered some
gowns," said Dunstan, lazily tapping his knee.

"Yes," replied Emily. "Half a dozen, I believe."

One of his bushy black eyebrows rose sharply
and Emily was immediately on the defensive
again. "I haven't had a new gown for a whole
year," she began, wishing that she didn't sound so
young and childish. "I did not exceed my quarterly
allowance either."

"No one has suggested that you did," replied
Dunstan with a look that one might give a naughty
child. "You will inform me when the gowns come,
as I intend to see them." He looked at her sharply. "I have been away at war," he said. "And so I
have been a little out of touch with the world of

the *haut ton*. Also, I have never approved of its addiction to certain addlepated notions of fashion. Therefore, I give you fair warning. If any of these new gowns are designed to be worn with damped petticoats, you may as well cancel them now."

In spite of all her efforts, Emily colored and glanced at Sarah. She had ordered one gown of the sheerest pale blue muslin, with the idea of damping her petticoat.

"But the ladies of the *ton*," she protested. "Surely they know what is right."

The viscount smiled, a cynical smile that did not reach his eyes. "In the first place, many of the ladies of the *ton* are not *ladies*. They may know what is right, but, if they do, they do not practice it. The damping of petticoats is a trick for an incognita, a means of puffing her charms. It is not for a decent woman."

Emily had no answer to this. Perhaps those incognitas had the right idea, she thought grimly, though she dared not say so. Such a woman could do as she pleased. Men paid for her favors. But for a decent woman marriage was the only course open, and marriage only meant that instead of obeying her father she obeyed her husband. To think that a woman must have a dowry, in order to get herself in such an unprofitable position! The world seemed cruelly unfair. Men had all the power.

Since Emily did not answer him, the viscount

rose from his chair and moved toward the big bed. "What does this pile contain? I haven't seen its contents."

Even Sarah flushed. "Milord, please. Those are Miss Penthorne's"—her voice fell to a low whisper —"nightdresses and—and—"

Since Sarah could not seem to get the word out, Emily spoke it. It resounded loudly in the quiet room. "Those are my new chemises, milord," she said. "And since no one sees them but myself I suppose they can be left to my discretion to choose. However," she watched his face carefully, hoping to score a hit, "we'll be glad to show them to you. Each one. I should never want to offend your sense of decency."

"Emily!" Poor Sarah's face had turned beet red.

"Why, Sarah, dear," replied Emily with exaggerated sweetness. "I am only trying to do as his lordship wishes."

Sarah shook her head and sighed, but the viscount regarded Emily steadily, a strange look in his eye. "I quite believe you are ready to do such an outlandish thing in the hope of embarrassing me." He smiled grimly. "Let me assure you, my dear, that the effort would be in vain. Ladies' chemises, whatever their design, are no novelty to me. As long as you wear yours, I shall leave their design to you."

"You are too kind, milord," Emily replied, the acid quality of her tone giving the lie to the acquiescent words. She felt the tears dangerously close and that made her even angrier. To cry before this impossible man would be absolutely humiliating.

"Miss Penthorne," he said.

"Yes, milord?"

"I quite realize that you are angry," he said evenly, his dark eyes regarding her coolly.

"How extremely astute of you!" Emily heard Sarah's gasp of dismay, but she was past the point of caring. This man was not only a tyrant, he had shattered the dream that she had been nourishing in her breast all winter. She could never think of marrying such a man—and certainly he would never imagine the possibility, seeing her as he did, as a sort of wayward child.

"Miss Penthorne," he began again, while she clenched her fists to keep back the tears. "I know that you are angry. I do hope that you understand. I do not harass you as a mere pastime. I am simply endeavoring to fulfill my duties to the best of my capacity. Surely you can understand that?"

There was a tone of almost pleading in his voice that touched Emily momentarily. But when Sarah nodded and said, "Of course, milord," some demon possessed Emily and she cried angrily, "I do not understand. I see only that you insist on treating me as a child—and a half-witted one, at that. It's—it's insulting, that's what it is!"

"Emily, you mustn't—"

The viscount silenced Sarah's remonstrance with an upraised hand. He looked at Emily sternly. "I treat you like a child," he said, "because you behave like one. Always angry and petulant."

Emily bristled up even more at this, but he continued. "However, you are young yet. Given time you will mature into a decent young woman, I've no doubt."

"And all because of your great guidance," flared Emily.

The viscount smiled slightly, the lazy laconic smile that the rakes affected. "I hope to have some part in the shaping of your character."

This was quite beyond the line and for a moment Emily was left speechless. Then she drew herself up and spoke with all the icy dignity she could muster. "I believe my character is quite sufficiently formed already. And until now I have heard no criticisms of it."

Dunstan eyed her for a minute and something in his look took her back to that first time—when she had noticed the stranger watching her from across the room. She felt herself color at the memory and wondered if the viscount remembered that evening. Surely he could not, for the look he had given her then had been frankly appreciative, the look of a man for a woman, not for a child.

His lordship turned to Sarah. "I am truly sorry to have so offended your charge. I have never be-

fore been responsible for—" He glanced quickly at
Emily. "A young woman. To be entirely truthful,
I suppose I should add that I find the responsibil-
ity rather galling."

"Milord." Emily, hearing the placating note in
her companion's voice, ground her teeth in anger. "Milord," Sarah went on. "I believe you. Emily
has not had the care of a really concerned guardian
—not that her Uncle Cyril does not care, but his
illness . . . She will eventually see that you are
doing the best for her."

Emily forced herself to remain silent. She knew
her anger had made her lose control of herself
in a way she never had before. She had behaved
childishly; she conceded that to herself. But she
couldn't help it. Every word he said to her, every
insulting, condescending, patronizing word seemed
specifically designed to infuriate her. Reason told
her that he did not intend that, but emotion insisted that she felt as though he did.

The viscount gave her once more quick glance
and then left the room.

"Emily, my dear," began Sarah as the door
closed behind him.

"Oh, Sarah, not now! I simply cannot bear another word. Please, please, just leave me be for a
while." And Emily, the tears finally released, threw
herself through the curtains onto the great bed
and began to sob and pound the pillow.

* * *

Sometime later there came a knock on the door. "Dinner," said Jeffers.

"Fine," replied Sarah. "We'll be right there."

Emily sat up and sniffled. "I do not care to eat," she told Sarah stiffly. "I am not hungry."

"But the viscount," Sarah began. "And your uncle."

"I do not care a pin how the viscount feels about it," replied Emily. "I am not hungry and I do not intend to go down to dinner. I shall see Uncle Cyril later—alone."

Sarah, in spite of her pleadings, was forced to go down to dinner alone. "I shall tell him you have a headache," she said at the door.

From her place on the bed Emily scowled. "I don't care what you tell him. I never want to think of that odious man again."

With a sigh Sarah closed the door behind her. Emily pounded the pillow again.

How she had looked forward to this trip. When the news of Napoleon's defeat and the coming Victory Celebration had arrived, more than half her joy had come from the knowledge that the sooner she returned to the city the sooner she would be able to begin the search for the man who possessed her heart. And now—now everything was utterly ruined. The wonderful, handsome man she had so longed for was an unspeakable tyrant who treated her abominably and who insisted on regarding her as a child. Not only

44

were her dreams of him shattered, but the chances of having any fun in the city were also ruined. She had thought Sarah stick-in-the-muddish. But this man . . . He was downright old-fashioned— and with the smuggest and most irritating belief that he knew everything.

Emily threw herself back against the pillows. How she hated it when he looked at her as he had. He made her feel that she was still in leading strings. It was unconscionable!

And to think how rude she had been to several perfectly nice young men last season, just because beside that romantic stranger they had seemed callow striplings. Well, she told herself sharply, if this was the behavior one could expect from a dark, romantic stranger, a stripling was much to be preferred.

Yet she had to admit that her memory of him had been quite accurate. His face was darkly handsome. There was something special about the way his hair curled over his collar. His shoulders were strong and broad and his inexpressibles, though not of the latest cut, showed a perfect leg. No, she decided. There had been no mistake in her picture of him. The mistake lay in not considering his character. That was it. How was she to know that the man who looked at her with such interest in his eyes would turn out to be a bully?

What if he had offered for her? Emily thought. What if he had offered last season and she had accepted? She would now be leg-shackled to a petty tyrant! She breathed a sigh of relief at her escape and was dismayed to find that her mind went on presenting her with pleasing pictures of herself and the viscount in an alliance.

How wonderful it would be to walk with her arm through his, to have him smile and say pleasant things to her as those young men had last year. But now—now it was highly unlikely that he would ever be more than polite to her.

She thumped the pillow once more. If only she could have known he was in that carriage. If only she had not looked at him for so long. But none of these "if-onlys" were of any value. The deed was done. He thought of her as a wayward child.

She threw the pillow against the far wall. In spite of the fact that that she had been slightly rude, his behavior had been insufferable!

## CHAPTER 4

The next morning Emily said good-bye to her Uncle Cyril with as much grace as possible. The poor man was quite ill and needed to go to Bath. She would simply have to deal with Dunstan herself.

For the next several days Emily and the viscount did not meet. He was usually gone from the house by the time she and Sarah rose, and he dined out. On the morning of the third day the new gowns arrived. Emily had Jeffers carry them up and then she indulged herself by trying them on, one after the other.

"They fit very well, don't they?" she asked Sarah as she eyed herself in the looking glass.

NINA PYKARE

"Very well," agreed Sarah, her eyes on the neckline of an evening dress of deep blue silk.

"I just love this color. Don't you think it looks well on me?"

"It does indeed," replied Sarah. "It brings out the blueness of your eyes. But the v—"

"Sarah." Emily's expression grew pained. "Don't spoil my fun by mentioning that odious man."

Sarah smiled gently. "Viscount Dunstan is your guardian and whether you like it or not you must face that fact. From now on, his wishes must be considered. I don't think he's going to like the neckline on that dress. I don't think he's going to like it at all."

Emily glanced downward. The dress was cut rather low, but perversely she did not admit it. "I saw gowns last season cut much lower—and on ladies of the *ton*."

Sarah sighed and shook her head. "You heard the viscount, Emily. He does not care about the ladies of the *ton*—or fashion either. He will simply go by his opinion. If I gamed at all, I would wager a pretty sum that he will not approve of this gown."

"But—" began Emily, when there came a smart tap on the door.

"Come in," called Sarah.

The door opened to reveal the viscount. "Ah," he said. "I was right. I just returned and Parks in-

48

formed me that the gowns had arrived. So I hurried up to get a look."

He smiled pleasantly at them both, almost as though he expected a smile in return, thought Emily angrily.

He strode across the room as though he owned it and stretched out his long form on a delicate lyre-back chair. "Please proceed," he said.

Emily pushed down her anger. Perhaps if she were nice to him . . . "This gown is for evening wear," she said, even managing a small smile. "Sarah says it brings out the blue in my eyes."

The viscount viewed her critically and nodded. "It does that, all right." Then his eyes fell on the neckline and he frowned. Emily felt herself redden as his gaze lingered there. For long moments there was silence and then he said, "The gown must go back."

"But milord—"

"There is no sense in trying to cozen me with smiles," replied Dunstan. "I cannot be swayed by such female machinations. The color is quite becoming, but the style is too old for you. The neckline . . ." His eyebrows drew together in a frown.

Emily felt the tears coming and Sarah intervened smoothly. "If it's only the neckline, milord, there are things that can be done. The gown is quite becoming. Why, I can sew in some lace. I have some in my sewing basket now. Let me show you."

Emily was forced to stand while Sarah tucked and pinned until his lordship decided that she was sufficiently covered. She knew she should be grateful to Sarah. Without her timely suggestion the gown would surely have been returned. But it was so infuriating to be treated like this that she could barely keep from screaming.

Finally his lordship nodded. "That should do. Let me see the others."

He pronounced the blue-sprigged muslin with little puffed sleeves and trailing blue ribbons all right. The green-sprigged, though cut differently, also earned his approval; so did the rose-spotted cambric and the green-striped sarcenet. Then Emily held her breath, for he had reached for the sky-blue muslin that she had intended to wear with a damped petticoat. The muslin was sheer, so sheer that she could see her hand through it.

He looked first at the neckline, but it seemed to be all right. Then he held up a piece of the material between them and the window. "This is a gown?"

"Yes, milord." Emily did her best to keep her tone conciliatory. Maybe, just maybe, he would let her keep it.

He cast her a suspicious glance. "This stuff is not dress material."

"Milord." Emily fought to keep calm. "The dressmaker said that every lady has at least one."

Dunstan snorted. "The dressmaker is like all

50

*modistes.* She makes her living by fashion. She would sell you anything that lined her pocket."

"When the gown is on, milord . . . over a petticoat . . ." Emily hated the pleading note in her voice, but she wanted that gown. Everything else about her trip to London was spoiled. It seemed vitally important to her to be able to keep this gown.

He frowned.

"Milord," said Sarah softly. "Emily does have a point. I mean, at least give her a chance to show you."

The viscount smiled pleasantly and something inside Emily lurched. Why could he never smile at *her* like that?

"Very well," he conceded. "Let her wear it for me." One eyebrow rose wickedly. "Perhaps I should have inspected her chemises," he said dryly. "With a gown like that, they will hardly be covered."

Sarah did not smile. "If you will step out into the hall, milord, I will help Emily change."

"I could just turn my back."

"Milord!" Sarah's plain face registered shock. "This is a young lady's bed chamber, not that of a— a—"

"Lightskirt," finished the viscount, not at all perturbed. "You must forgive my breach of etiquette. My years on the town and my years at the front have ill prepared me for dealing with young ladies. I much appreciate your calling me to task."

The viscount's voice was entirely serious, but Emily, glancing at Sarah, saw that she, too, was unsure that he meant it. Evidently the viscount realized this. "I mean what I say, Miss Sarah. I intend to do everything I can to fulfill my duties as well as possible. Any assistance you can give me will be much appreciated."

"I will give you every assistance I can," said Sarah soberly. "Emily is quite dear to me."

His lordship nodded. "That is evident. I shall wait in the hall till you summon me." He shook his head. "Though I must tell you that your efforts will probably be futile. That material . . ."

He shut the door.

"Quick, Sarah, my heaviest petticoat."

Sarah eyed her charge skeptically. "Only if you give me your word that you will wear the gown with that petticoat and no other. I do not intend to help you bamboozle his lordship."

"Yes, Sarah, yes. I promise. But I want this gown. You know I do. Now help me, please."

Sarah gave her charge a quick smile. "Of course I'll help you, my dear." Her hands reached for the hooks on the back of Emily's dress.

In a matter of minutes they had found the heavy petticoat and Emily had slipped it on. "Oh, Sarah, it's such a lovely gown."

52

"Yes, it is," agreed Sarah. "But the stuff is very fine."

"Sarah!"

Sarah patted Emily's hand. "Now, Emily, calm down. You must hold to your ladylike deportment. You see his lordship can be amenable."

Emily nodded. "Yes, yes, Sarah, I see. But, oh, I do want this gown."

"Yes, dear." Sarah's hands sped over the gown, smoothing here, tucking there. "It does look lovely. Are you ready?"

Emily nodded, but as Sarah turned to open the door her charge moved quickly so that his lordship would be between her and the light. She held her breath as he entered. Except for the sheerness of the muslin the gown was quite demure. Its rounded neck exposed nothing. Its sleeves, emerging from little puffs at the shoulders, clung closely to the wrists, where they were edged in self-ruffles. The high-gathered bodice was banded underneath by a long sash of the same material which tied in the back and flared out behind.

The viscount resumed his chair and regarded her closely. "Walk around a little," he said.

She felt the color rising as she complied. Every time he looked at her like this, with that speculative look in his eye, she felt the quickening of her breath as she had that night at Lady Cholmondoley's ball.

When he was angry it was different. Then she felt like a little girl who had been extremely bad—in some way she did not quite understand.

But now when he wasn't angry, when he looked at her as a man looks at a woman, her heart fluttered, her breath quickened, and she felt grown up and exciting in a way she had never felt with those callow young striplings who were so fond of paying her extravagant and unoriginal compliments. She had barely refrained from laughing in their faces when they repeated the same old stuff about skin like lilies and lips like roses.

But with Dunstan it was very different. If he had ever told her either of those things, she would have been thrilled.

When he had agreed before that blue was becoming to her, she had forgotten that she was angry with him, forgotten that he was a bully and a tyrant, forgotten everything except that wonderful, exciting feeling she had first experienced when she found his eyes upon her that night at the ball.

The viscount continued to regard her critically and she felt the heated blood fill her cheeks.

"I cannot decide," he said. "Stand over there by the window. The light is better there."

Emily obeyed, but her heart fell. In the sunlight the sheer, filmy material would be almost transparent. Still, there was little else to do. If

Dunstan wanted to see the dress in the sunlight, he would. She could be quite sure of that.

Finally he shook his head. "This one must go back."

"Milord . . ." Emily's voice was a wail.

"I am truly sorry," he said, and his face seemed to indicate it. "But the gown is too old for you." He raised a hand to still her protest. "There is no use in complaining. I considered it from every angle. I have been quite fair. But it just will not do. I'll see that your account is credited. Order yourself another gown."

Emily blinked rapidly to keep back the tears. She refused to cry in front of him. Nor would she beg anymore. She was through trying to please him. She turned her back on him and looked out the window. She would not cry, she told herself severely. There were flowers out there; she tried to count the kinds to keep her mind on something besides her anger and her hurt.

"Send the gown to me," she heard him tell Sarah. "And the direction of the *modiste*." His tone sobered. "I wish to have a talk with her."

"Yes, milord," said Sarah.

Emily continued to stare out the window until she heard the door close behind him. Then she turned, her eyes blinded with tears. Without a word, Sarah helped her out of the gown. Emily did not trust herself to speak until the gown was safely off. Then, still wearing the petticoat, she stamped her foot. "He's a beast, Sarah, a terrible beast!"

"Now, Emily, you are being unfair to the viscount," soothed Sarah. "He really is concerned for your welfare."

"I don't believe that," cried Emily, by now completely distraught. "He hates me. I know he does. And I hate him! I hate him with all my heart and soul!"

## CHAPTER 5

When Emily went down to breakfast the next morning, she was still angry. She was not quite sure if her anger was caused entirely by the viscount's insistence on returning her favorite gown. She was also angered, perhaps even more than by that incident, by his refusal to recognize her as a woman. It was insupportable that she should be so aware of him as a woman and so afflicted by that awareness and that he should insist upon seeing her only as a recalcitrant child.

As she approached the breakfast room, she was surprised by the sound of footsteps behind her. She turned. "Milord." Emily was aware that color flooded her face at the sight of him.

"I did not mean to startle you," he said, as if he

had never thwarted and insulted her. "I thought I heard your steps on the stairs and I came to tell you myself."

"Tell me what?" asked Emily, fighting her anger and her feelings for him.

"I have rented a box at the theater for tonight. To see Kean as Othello." He paused to see how she would respond.

"I hope you enjoy yourself," she replied perversely.

His face hardened. "You mistake me, Miss Penthorne. I rented a box for you and your companion to accompany me. Kean is all the rage now and this is his first time performing *Othello*. I thought perhaps you would enjoy seeing him. Also, it will give you a chance to be seen." He eyed her sternly. "I believe you have come to London in search of a husband. That is the usual course for a young woman of your age."

"Of course," she replied stiffly. "The sooner you find me a husband, the sooner you will be relieved of the irksome and galling responsibility of being my guardian."

His eyes raked her over. "Quite so. You are most astute. Kindly be ready for the theater on time. Since I am not one of those who go merely to be gawked at, I wish to see the play from its beginning." Without waiting for her answer, he strode off.

Emily stood trembling for several minutes. Why

had she let her anger get the best of her? Certainly that had been a conciliatory gesture on his part. She had dreamed all winter of being in London, of going to the theater on the arm of a man. She had even dreamed of being with this man. But how different her dream had been. In it he had smiled and praised her beauty. Then she had smiled and clung to his arm.

But it would not be like that. The way he was acting they would be at cuffs all evening. And they were going to see Kean.

She turned toward the stairs and Sarah. The blue silk dress. She must ask Sarah to fix it, to put the lace in. He had said he liked her in blue. Maybe, just maybe if she kept her temper under control, if just this once she did everything the way he wanted it . . . She lifted her skirts and hurried upstairs.

By the time evening came, Emily had almost forgotten her anger in her excitement. Sarah had put the lace in the blue gown, quite high enough to please anyone. Emily's hair had been tousled and teased into a mass of tangled curls that approximated the newest à la Titus fashion. She stood before the cheval glass and looked at herself critically. The deep blue gown fit snugly across the bodice and fell from its gathers in graceful folds to the floor. She did not look like a child, she told herself proudly. Anyone with half a brain could see that she was a woman—a full-grown woman.

She checked the lace at the bodice; it must cover everything. Of course, she had looked more grown up before its addition.

Jewels—that was it. The dress needed just the right jewels. She turned to go ask Sarah, but then stopped. Her companion was busy getting ready. She had spent a great deal of time in dressing Emily and now she would have to hurry to be ready on time herself.

Emily moved toward the chest and her jewel box. She would pick out something herself, something that would make her look older. She opened the chest that held her mother's jewels.

What would an older woman wear to the theater? She lifted out her mother's emeralds, but they did not go with the dress. She considered the opals and the tourmalines, then shook her head. No, they would not do. And then she saw them. The very thing! The diamonds. That ought to convince him.

She hurried to the cheval glass and fastened the swinging diamonds onto her earlobes, put the gleaming pendant around her neck, and clasped the bracelet around her gloved wrist. There, now let him tell her that she wasn't a woman.

She grabbed up her cashmere and hurried to Sarah's room. She tapped at the door. "I'm not quite ready, Emily," called Sarah through the door. "Go down so as to keep his lordship from being angered at you."

"Yes, Sarah. Right away."

Emily threw the shawl over the arm and moved carefully down the stairs. No higgledy-piggledy scurrying for a grown-up lady. She held her head high and moved as gracefully as she could.

She was near the bottom of the stairs when she heard the viscount approaching. His eyes were upon her as she finished the descent and she smiled at him. "Good evening, milord." Her hand moved to her bodice where his eyes lingered. "Sarah fixed my gown. Does it meet with your approval?"

She asked the question lightly, in a bantering tone, and so was not prepared for the sternness of his reply.

"I see that. The gown is quite adequate. The jewels are not."

"These are my mama's diamonds," she replied.

"It's too bad that your mama is not here to advise you that young women do not go about blazing like that."

"My mama has been dead these three years," she replied over the lump in her throat. "She did not instruct me in the wearing of jewels."

"Your companion should have known better. Innocent young women do not wear diamonds."

Emily swallowed again. "Sarah did not see me. She was still dressing and sent me on without her so I would not be late."

"That explains it." The viscount regarded her soberly. "If you hurry, you can change your jewels in time."

Emily stared at him, her anger rising again. Must he always be right?

"Go now and change," he repeated. "Have you a string of pearls, one strand?"

Emily nodded.

"Put them on. Them and nothing else. Do you understand?"

Emily nodded. She did not trust herself to speak; the tears were too close. Why was everything she did going wrong? She had meant to make him notice that she was a woman and instead she had convinced him more than ever that she was an irresponsible child. The tears rose to her eyes and she blinked rapidly. She could not cry now. There was no time. Besides, she must be able to see to find the pearls.

Pearls! Only schoolroom misses wore pearls. But she put the diamonds away and fastened the pearls. She could not understand why he wanted her to wear pearls, but she wanted to be with him, so she wiped the tears from her eyes and hurried back down the stairs.

He stood where she had left him, and for the first time she noticed what he was wearing. His new coat of corbeau color with covered buttons accented the breadth of his shoulders. His inexpressibles of sage-green kerseymere clung to an admirable leg. His waistcoat was of white marcella and his cravat boasted the mathematical tie. All in all, he was a fine figure of a man. A prime article, as Cousin Percy would say. Fleetingly Emily wondered how the ebullient Percy was faring at Cambridge.

Then the viscount spoke. "That's better. You look like a young woman your age should look—very lovely."

Emily felt the color rush to her cheeks. "Thank you, milord. You look quite nice yourself."

The viscount gave her a surprised smile. "Thank you." He flicked an imaginary speck of dust from his sleeve. "My tailor did an excellent job. He was recommended to me by the Beau."

"Beau Brummell?" asked Emily.

Dunstan nodded. "Yes, I ran into him at White's the other day."

Emily found herself staring at him. He looked so fine. If only there were not so much anger between them.

His eyes met hers and seemed to probe them. It was almost as though he sought some knowledge there, the answer to some question. He seemed about to say something to her and then the sound of Sarah's voice came floating down the stairs. "Milord, I am sorry to keep you waiting."

Dunstan turned to greet her. "Good evening, Miss Parker. We shall be quite on time if we leave now."

"Thank you, milord. You are very kind."

The viscount shook his head. "Miss Penthorne and I have been having a little talk. Getting to know each other better."

Emily gave him a surprised glance. He had not mentioned the diamonds at all. He was smiling at her pleasantly, quite as though they had never quarreled.

He reached out and took her shawl. "The carriage should be waiting out front. Allow me."

He put the shawl carefully around her shoulders and just as carefully adjusted it. Emily felt a shiver through her. How often in the last winter had she dreamed of such a scene—except that in her dreams she had taken his lordship's arm and smiled up at him with eyes full of adoration, a thing she dared not do now.

Then he turned to Sarah, but she had already managed her shawl.

Emily noticed little of the city during the trip to Drury Lane. She was too busy drinking in the presence of this new viscount. He could really be quite charming when he was not playing the over-zealous guardian. She wondered idly how many hearts he had broken before he went away to the wars. Then her own heart gave a great lurch in her breast. Perhaps he loved someone. Perhaps he only waited to get her off his hands to marry himself. Her heart thudded in her throat.

But then she calmed herself. He had just returned to London after many years away. He had no time to form a partiality for anyone. And besides that, she told herself grimly, it didn't matter. The viscount might make whatever alliance he pleased. It was of no concern to her.

A sick feeling invading her stomach at this thought immediately contradicted it. Well, she told herself stubbornly, there was nothing she could do about it that night. She would simply enjoy Kean.

# CHAPTER 6

As they neared Drury Lane the streets grew more and more crowded. The hoarse cries of coachmen jockeying for position resounded through the air and now and then an oath could be heard. One of these was particularly profane and Emily saw Sarah flinch. His lordship, however, appeared not to notice.

"I hope you will enjoy seeing *Othello*," he said. "This is Kean's first appearance in the part." He frowned. "I hope he does it justice. Critics have long held that there is no character for which a good voice and a fine figure are more indispensably requisite than Othello. And Kean is certainly not a man of great stature."

"Have you seen him do Iago?" inquired Sarah.

Dunstan nodded. "Yes, several times. He is quite superb in the part. The man is a born actor, there's no denying that. But Othello—I hope we shall not be disappointed."

"The crush in the street seems terrible," said Emily. "I do not remember it being like this last year."

"Most probably it was not," agreed his lordship. "As I said, this is Kean's first time in the part. He is quite the rage this year. Some say the man will rival the great Garrick."

From what she had read, this hardly seemed possible to Emily. Everyone knew that Garrick had been the greatest actor in the history of the theater. "What do you think, milord?"

The viscount smiled. "I am withholding my judgment until I have seen more of the man's work. There is no disputing the fact that he is excellent." The carriage came to a halt. "Well, here we are. And half of London, too, it appears. Kean is a great favorite."

He opened the carriage door and preceded them out. As she laid her gloved hand in his, Emily felt herself color again, but fortunately no one could see.

Around them the press of people crowded. In the light of the torches Emily surveyed the crowd. Everywhere diamonds blazed. They dripped from the ears, throats, and wrists of richly dressed women. They shone from the noble decorations adorning the chests of spendidly dressed men. Emily had never seen so many gems. Her hand moved self-consciously to her throat and the single strand of pearls. Amid all this brilliance she looked even more the schoolroom miss.

The viscount took her arm in his and shouldered a passageway through the crowd while Sarah followed closely.

The inside of Drury Lane was a little less crowded, but almost as noisy. His lordship led them up the stairs to a nicely decorated box. "There," he said as he seated them. "We shall be able to get a good view of Kean and let others get a good view of us." He frowned. "The *ton* has more than one custom that I find quite annoying. Among them is the pernicious habit of ogling one another. One would think the theater had been built for that express purpose." He turned a stern face to Emily. "Should your eye happen to meet that of some smart young buck, simply cut him dead. I trust you know how to do that."

"Yes, milord," replied Emily. "But isn't it natural for people to want to be looked at? I mean, here are crowds of people all dressed up. Of course they want to be noticed. It is only human."

The viscount considered this. "Perhaps you are right. But at any rate, do not exchange glances with any young oglers. Most of the bucks are merely amusing themselves. If a man wants to consider an alliance with you, he can do it in the proper way—by calling."

Emily did not reply to this. She was lost in the memory of the first time she had exchanged glances with a man—with his lordship himself. She felt her cheeks warm at the memory of the speculation in his eyes.

"Emily," said Sarah. "Emily, his lordship just asked you something."

Color stained Emily's cheeks again. "I—I was daydreaming. I'm sorry."

"I merely inquired if you should like an orange."

Emily shook her head. "I think not," she said. "I'm afraid the juice may stain my new gown."

The viscount nodded. "And you, Miss Sarah?"

"No, thank you, milord. I am fine."

As the two talked, Emily allowed her eyes to travel over the pit. Everything looked as usual there. Orange girls were hawking their wares, smiling roguishly at their customers. Now there, thought Emily with a suppressed smile, there were bodices to remonstrate about. Even at this distance it was easy to see that the orange girls' bodices used the very minimum of material. Her imagination flashed her a picture of his lordship's outraged expression should he find her in such a bodice. Then the blood rushed to her face again at the thought of his eyes lingering there.

Once more she concentrated on the antics of

the bucks in the pit. Some strolled nonchalantly about parading their finery. Others cracked nuts with gusto or ate oranges and tossed the peels gaily over their shoulders.

Emily raised her eyes from the pit to the boxes across the theater. There sat the beautifully clad ladies of the *ton*. Jewels blazed from ears and wrists, and from above necklines cut much lower than hers had been without the lace. She considered pointing this out to the viscount, but then thought better of it. They were dealing together reasonably well at the moment. She wanted it to remain that way.

Slowly Emily let her gaze move around the boxes. In one, surrounded by elegant and attentive men, sat an auburn-haired beauty whose only jewels were long emerald earrings. Her pale shoulders rose above a dress of cream-colored satin. Emily was just about to ask Dunstan about her when she recognized one of the other women in the box. She was one of those Sarah and she had seen in the carriage the day they arrived in London, one of the young women Sarah had said were incognitas. So the auburn-haired one must be an incognita, too, and rather a well-liked one, it seemed from the look of things.

Emily was suddenly startled by seeing the woman nod in her direction and she turned toward Dunstan just in time to see him incline his head slightly. Her heart jumped into her throat.

71

Dunstan knew that woman! Perhaps she had even belonged to him. The thought made her tremble. Compared to such a woman, what had she to offer Dunstan? Beside such a woman she was just a chit. She was consumed with curiosity, but she dared not ask his lordship who the woman was.

She forced herself to consider the rest of the theater. The women were certainly richly dressed and bedecked with jewels. She studied the women in several boxes, trying to deduce their status. Were they ladies of the *ton* or incognitas? There was simply no way to tell. All were richly dressed and bejeweled and all carried their heads quite high.

Perhaps there was another way, thought Emily, intrigued by the puzzle she had set herself. Perhaps she could learn more about the status of the ladies from the conduct of the gentlemen. First she studied those in the box of the known incognitas. One and all, the gentlemen were polite and quite attentive, eagerly hanging on to the ladies' words.

In several other boxes she noticed similar activity among the gentlemen. But in most boxes the case was otherwise. The ladies and gentlemen both appeared bored, and both seemed much more interested in quizzing those around them. Emily could not help recalling her comment to

Sarah that the incognitas seemed very content. How strange that such reprehensible ladies appeared to enjoy life a great deal while the decent ones did not.

She was still mulling this over when the great curtain rose. Emily leaned forward to see and hear better. As Iago revealed his treachery to his master Othello in the words, "I follow him to serve my turn upon him," she shivered. The treachery of Iago was beyond belief. For a simple man like Othello to penetrate such dissimulation was too difficult.

Emily's heart ached for the gentle Desdemona, lured into loving this simple giant. Kean was not a large man, yet he appeared big and warriorlike. At first she might have agreed with Brabantio that nothing short of witchcraft could have made his daughter love such a man as Othello, yet before very long she had entirely forgotten Kean's stature. Caught up in the magic of the play, she did not realize that the man beside her spent more time watching her face than he did the stage.

When the curtain fell for intermission, Emily had a hard time re-entering the world of reality. "Oh," she breathed in answer to Dunstan's questioning look. "He's everything they say he is."

His lordship smiled dryly. "Well, the managers must be quite pleased. He is certainly bringing in a good gate." He turned to Sarah. "The bucks and beaus will soon be trampling down the door to meet Miss Penthorne here. Before they start arriving, I believe I should warn you."

Sarah looked confused. "Warn me? Of what, milord?"

"Among them will be a certain Viscount Bersford, an old friend of mine. And of yours."

Emily, watching this exchange, was shocked to see her friend turn white. "Sarah! Are you ill?"

"No, no. I—I am just a little—taken aback."

"Aware as I am of the connection that once existed between you, I did not think it wise to let him come upon you unannounced."

"Yes." Sarah nodded weakly. "That was most kind of you."

"Sarah!" Emily was quite concerned over her friend's reaction. "Who is this Bersford? What is the viscount talking about?"

Sarah raised a trembling hand to her lips. "Lord Bersford and I—we were about to be promised when Papa lost everything. The match was never made. I released Bersford from his promise and he went away to fight."

"Oh," cried Emily. "How dreadful of him to behave like that. I suppose he then married some heiress."

His lordship intervened. "*Au contraire*. Bersford made no alliance."

Sarah started and clutched her shawl. "No alliance?"

74

"That is correct," said his lordship.

"I still think his behavior was reprehensible," said Emily. "If I loved someone, I should not let anyone stop me from being with him."

"You are not a man," replied his lordship. "With a man's responsibilities."

"I don't care," protested Emily. "Love is more important than money. Much more important."

"What do you know of love?" Dunstan asked sharply.

Under the scrutiny of those dark eyes Emily flushed. "I—I know that it's important. I know that."

The viscount looked relieved. She must not let him suspect that she had spent the winter hopelessly in love with a man. Not when he was that man.

The door to the box opened. "I say, Dunstan," drawled a lazy voice. "Who is that gem?"

From the expression on Dunstan's face it was clear that he did not regard this man as a friend. "Hello, Gilcrest. This is my Uncle Cyril's ward, Miss Penthorne. I am presently serving as her guardian."

"Ah-ha! I win my wager." As Lord Gilcrest moved farther into the light, Emily saw a tall fair man with a lean, sharp face. "Pleased to meet you, Miss Penthorne," he said, raising her gloved hand to his lips.

"Lord Gilcrest," she murmured, wondering how

long the two men could stay in close proximity without coming to cuffs. They were obviously at odds over something and only the dictates of polite society kept them from tangling with each other.

Fortunately the door to the box opened again to admit a stream of beaus, all of whom exclaimed over Emily's beauty.

In spite of the fact that she was thus occupied, Emily couldn't help noticing that Sarah's eyes turned constantly to the door. And then, just as she was receiving some silly compliment about the whiteness of her skin, Dunstan looked up and said, "Bersford! Come in, man. Come in."

Emily, her eyes flying to Sarah's face, saw her friend blanch even more; then the man moved into the box. "My ward, Miss Penthorne," said Dunstan. "And her companion, Miss Parker."

Bersford's eyes looked deep into Sarah's. "I already have the pleasure of knowing Miss Parker. How are you?"

Somehow the question seemed far too personal and Emily waited for her friend to put the man in his place.

"I am fine, fine," Sarah replied, a break in her voice belying the word.

Then Emily's attention was drawn back to the line of men in front of her and she had little time to watch Sarah. She was surprised, however, to find when the box emptied out that Lord Bersford had remained.

"If you would care to join us," invited Dunstan. Bersford looked toward Sarah, and Emily saw her companion give the briefest of nods.

"Thank you, Dunstan. I shall do that."

As Bersford pulled up a chair next to Sarah, Emily studied the man. He was of the same height as Dunstan, but there the similarity ended. In looks the viscount's friend was nondescript. He was not ugly, but he had none of the rakish good looks that characterized Dunstan. Bersford was a plain, hearty-looking man. Nothing about him to make her heart beat fast, thought Emily. How could Sarah still love a man who had left her like that?

But, then, love was a strange business. It was certainly not sensible for her to love Dunstan, knowing his character as she did.

It was obvious that Sarah did still care for this man. Emily had never seen her cousin so distraught. Sarah twisted her lace handkerchief until it was almost in shreds. Her eyes shone with unusual brilliance, and they seemed always to be drawn to his face as she hung onto his every word.

Emily moved to edge her chair closer. This *tête-à-tête* could not be good for Sarah. The viscount's hand on her chair stopped her. He leaned closer to whisper in her ear. "Your friend is entitled to some privacy."

"But—but I do not want her to be hurt again," protested Emily.

The viscount patted her gloved hand. "You can't stop her from being hurt. Nor anyone else you love. Hurting is a condition of being alive."

"But he left her," said Emily.

"He was young and he had parents who controlled his purse strings. You do not understand the difficulties of being a man."

Emily met the dark eyes so near her own. "Men always think that life is more difficult for them. But they have control over their lives. Women do not."

Dunstan's eyes probed deep into hers again, as though for an answer to something. "Women are weak. They need protection. They cannot care for themselves."

Something inside Emily snapped. "That's not true. Women can take care of themselves. Look at that woman over there—the one with the auburn hair. She takes care of herself."

Dunstan frowned fiercely. "That is Harriette Wilson, London's leading demi-rep. It is from a life like hers that marriage will protect you."

In her anger Emily forgot all propriety. "So for the privilege of being protected from a terrible life like hers—" She cast a glance across the theater where the infamous woman was laughing pleasantly. "I must give up control of my life to my husband."

Dunstan frowned. "That is the custom."

"The custom is odious," protested Emily. "It makes women mere slaves."

Dunstan eyed her closely. "I think you have forgotten one consideration."

"And that is?"

"Love."

"Love!" Emily snorted. "How many marriages are really made for love? Look out there." She gestured imperiously. "I bet I can tell you whether the boxes contain ladies or—or other women." Why couldn't she just say incognita, she thought angrily. It wasn't such a difficult word to say. "Do you know how I can tell?"

He shook his head. "No."

"The ladies look universally bored and unhappy. And the—the incognitas—" There, she had got the word out. "The incognitas look happy."

Dunstan's eyes quickly surveyed the crowd and swung back to her. "Your perception is rather accurate, I must admit. At least on the surface. But looks can be deceiving."

"Perhaps." Emily would only concede so much. She found suddenly that being so close to him had quickened her breath again. What if he read her feelings in her look? She wrenched her eyes away and gazed once more across the theater.

As she did so, her glance was caught and held by a fair, lean man—Gilcrest. She remembered him because of the obvious tension that had existed between him and Dunstan. Gilcrest's eyes were frankly speculative, as Dunstan's had been that night at Lady Cholmondoley's ball.

Suddenly the man beside her moved. "I thought I expressly asked you not to exchange glances with the beaus," he said harshly.

"But it's Lord Gilcrest," protested Emily. "I just met him. Besides, if I am forbidden even to look around, how am I to find a husband?"

"You have a peculiar conception of how one achieves that," he said sternly. "At any rate, bucks the like of Gilcrest are not good husband material."

"I don't see why not," said Emily innocently. "He's a lord. He has good blood."

"He also has an overabundance of debts," returned the viscount curtly. "Which he might like to pay off with your fortune."

"I thought that was the fashion," replied Emily, continuing her role of innocent.

"As I said when we were discussing clothes, what is fashionable may well not be right. I have no intention of letting you marry such a man."

"But if I love him?"

The viscount absolutely glared at her. "I should hope you would have better understanding than to love a man like that."

Emily shrugged. "And what sort of man should I marry?" she inquired far too sweetly.

"Hopefully someone with a little common sense who would not game away your portion and leave you destitute."

"Lord Gilcrest does not look destitute," she protested, driven to harass him in this manner by some urge she did not understand.

"Of course he does not. The man is not foolish enough to go about proclaiming his insolvent condition to the world, especially if he is looking for a wife to ease his financial difficulties."

"And how do you know all this?" inquired Emily.

The viscount smiled cynically. "First, Gilcrest frequents White's. I have been present when he lost great sums of money there. Second, my tailor complained to me of him when last I paid my reckoning. When a man like Gilcrest so neglects his tailor—any sensible person takes note."

"I see," agreed Emily. She was wondering if she dared ask the reason for this so evident concern of his, but the curtain rose again and she returned her attention to the stage and poor Othello, feeling the tears rise to her eyes at his unfounded suspicion and murder of the woman whose only crime was loving him.

The journey home was quite pleasant. Sarah seemed very happy, bantering with his lordship in a way she had never done before. There was no more unpleasantness between Emily and Dunstan.

In fact, sitting beside him in the carriage, Emily could almost believe that her dreams had come true.

When they reached the house on St. James's Square, he handed her down with as much gentleness as any man with a partiality for a lady. Going up the walk on his arm, she wished that she could make this moment last forever.

At the foot of the stairs he turned to Sarah. "I hope you enjoyed the evening as much as I did."

"I did, milord. I enjoyed it very much." Sarah's eyes were still brilliant and her voice held a buoyancy that was new to Emily's ears.

The viscount smiled gravely. "I am glad that you and my friend Bersford have settled your differences so amicably."

"We had no differences," Sarah was quick to reply. "It was Bersford's parents who objected." The smile faded from her face. "They will still object."

"Do not let that cause you alarm," his lordship said. "Bersford is a man now. He knows what he wants and it is not a rich heiress."

Sarah's face turned rosy. "You are very kind, milord. Very kind."

Dunstan shook his head. "I've seen Bersford through many a scrap. He's been a sort of younger brother to me. I'm very pleased to see him so happy."

Sarah flushed again at this and muttered another thank you before she turned and went up the stairs. Emily gave his lordship a smile that reflected her pleasure in his concern for her friend. "Good night, milord."

"Good night, Emily."

Something in the tone of his voice, something almost like a caress, caused her to tremble violently. Somehow as she turned, she caught her toe in the hem of her gown and tripped. She would have fallen right at his feet if the viscount had not reached out and caught her in his strong arms.

She came up against his white marcella waistcoat with a thump that quite knocked the breath from her body. "Oh!" The word was jolted from her.

For several moments he kept her there against his chest. She got her breath back, but then she lost it again. The strength of his arms around her, the sound of his heart beating under her ear, the warmth of his body close to hers, all combined to leave her breathless. She fought the urge to move closer, to burrow into his arms.

Then he put her from him gently and smiled down at her gravely. "I hope you did not suffer any injury."

Emily shook her head. "No, milord. I am—fine." His face was very close to hers and she felt her heart thudding in her throat. She knew she should wrench her eyes away, but something in his held her captive.

Then he spoke again. "Sleep well, Emily."

There it was, that strange caressing tone to his voice. "You, too, milord," she managed to mumble before she turned and made her way up the stairs, feeling as though her slippers barely touched the carpet.

# CHAPTER 7

When Emily woke the next morning, she stretched and smiled. She had rather enjoyed their trip to the theater in spite of the slight altercation with Dunstan. Curiously she wondered what it was that made his lordship so angry with Gilcrest. After all, one could not go to the theater without being ogled. Anyone knew that. And other men had ogled her in the course of the evening.

Then she thought of that tender moment when she had almost fallen. Could it be possible that that look last winter had meant something? Could his lordship really care for her? His actions of the night before could be taken that way. Of course, she had to stretch things a little to do it. Oh, why couldn't he see her as a woman? Why?

She sat up and swung her legs over the side of the bed. There was no use thinking such thoughts, they would only make her sad again. And, really, she had a lot to be happy about. She and Dunstan had dealt well together last night. Perhaps they could do better now. Perhaps they needn't always be at cuffs with each other.

She would get up and have her breakfast. The sun was shining through the window. It looked like it would be a lovely day, too lovely a day to spend mooning about inside.

She clapped her hands. That was it! She would ask Sarah to go shopping again. Of course she would be very careful. She would only buy things that she was sure he would approve. Perhaps she would not buy anything, but just get out in the fresh air and sunshine, see a few people. She felt a real need to move around.

She put on a dress of yellow-sprigged muslin, ran a brush through her tangled curls, and went to find Parks and order the carriage. This was going to be a very good day.

"Parks, oh, Parks," she called as she almost skipped down the stairs.

"Yes, miss." The butler smiled at her obvious good spirits.

"Oh, Parks. It's such a lovely day. Please order the carriage round. Sarah and I are going shopping."

Parks's face changed rapidly, his smile fading to be replaced by a look of dismay. "Ah, miss—"

"Yes, Parks. What is it?"

"It's the carriage, miss. I can't order it round."

"Why not? Has his lordship taken it?"

"No, miss." The old butler shook his head.

"Then the carriage is here."

"Yes, miss."

"Then order it round." Emily was getting confused. There was obviously something that Parks didn't want to tell her. "All right, Parks," she demanded. "Will you tell me plainly why I cannot have the carriage?"

"Yes, miss." The servitor hesitated. "It's—it's because of his lordship. His lordship said . . ." It was plain that he didn't want to continue, but Emily stared at him until he did. "His lordship said you weren't to have the carriage without his permission." Parks looked highly uncomfortable.

"He what?" Emily knew that her voice had risen shrilly.

"He said you weren't to have the carriage without his permission."

"And when did he say this?"

"Just this morning in the library, miss."

"I see." Emily forced herself to remain calm. "Thank you, Parks. That will be all."

"Yes, miss." Parks was clearly glad to be dismissed.

For a moment Emily stood, not believing what she had heard. Just when she thought things were going well between them, he did a terrible thing like this. She had always had a carriage at her disposal. He had no right, no right at all, to forbid her the use of it. She would tell him so.

She strode off angrily toward the library. This kind of behavior was absolutely insupportable.

At the library door she paused and then, taking a deep breath, pushed it open. "Milord, this has got to—"

Emily stopped suddenly. The library was empty.

She stormed out and down the hall. "Parks! Parks! Where are you?"

The aged butler hurried into the hall. "Yes, miss. Right here, miss."

Emily strove to speak calmly, but her anger was so great that she had trouble getting the words out. "Parks, where is the viscount? I wish to speak to him."

"His lordship is out on business."

"And when will he return?" asked Emily.

"I don't know, miss. He didn't say, but he's often gone all day."

"I see." Emily had to swallow twice before she could continue. "Please inform me as soon as his lordship arrives home. I have a matter to discuss with him."

"Yes, miss. Right away, miss."

Emily nodded and turned to go upstairs. She must find Sarah. She would burst if she couldn't talk to someone. Angrily she stamped down the hall toward Sarah's room and pushed open the door. "Sarah! Sarah! You'll never know what that terrible man has done now."

Sarah looked up from where she was needle-pointing a firescreen. "Emily, Emily, my dear. Whatever is the matter?"

"It's Dunstan. Oh, Sarah." Emily paced the room angrily. "It's such a lovely day. I wanted to go shopping. I went to Parks to order the carriage. And—and he said—" She stopped and faced her cousin. "He said I couldn't have the carriage without his lordship's permission." Tears of anger rolled down her cheeks as Emily resumed her pacing.

"Now, Emily. Please, dear. Calm down. The viscount means well. You know he does. Last night he was very considerate."

"I know, I know. That's what makes it so terrible. Last night he was so nice. And today—to do this to me today. Oh, Sarah, I hate him. I really do."

"Now, Emily."

Emily stamped her foot. "Do not treat me like a little child, Sarah. This is a terrible thing he has done. So humiliating." She stamped her foot again. "He's an odious, odious man."

Sarah laid aside her needlework. "Some of what

he says is true," she replied evenly. "At times you do behave childishly. I do not understand it myself. You were never quite like this before."

"It's him!" Emily wrung her hands. "He drives me to distraction."

"It's easy to see that," Sarah continued. "The question in my mind is why."

For a moment Emily stopped her pacing. Dear God, Sarah must not know the truth. "I don't see anything strange about it," she said. "He's so high and mighty. He treats me abominably."

"Perhaps he is a little high-handed," admitted Sarah. "But I really do believe he means the best for you."

"I'm sure you do," replied Emily. "After all, he's been exceptionally kind to you."

Sarah's face turned rosy red. "Emily! I would not let the viscount's treatment of me influence my concern for you."

Sarah looked so genuinely hurt that Emily hurried contritely to her side. "Oh, Sarah, I know that. I truly do. It's just—I feel like a prisoner. And I don't even know what I'm being punished for!"

Sarah shook her head. "I know it is hard for you, dear. You have never really been disciplined. But perhaps you will find a husband soon, and then you will be free of the viscount."

"Perhaps," replied Emily, but she knew that such freedom would never be hers. For in spite of the intensity of her anger at him, she had still seen no man to match him. There was no man in all London—in all the world—who could usurp the place the terrible viscount held in her heart.

It was not a happy thought and Emily made her excuses to Sarah and went to the back courtyard where she expended some of her energy in weeding the flower beds. Since much of the time her vision was blurred by scalding tears and since she neglected to provide herself with gloves or an apron, in the ensuing hour she brought more havoc than order to the flower beds and to her own person.

The yellow-sprigged muslin grew stained and her hands became stiff and unsightly, swollen from such unusual activity and contact with the dirt. Still she continued in her self-imposed task. She simply had to do something.

She had just wrestled with a particularly stubborn, long-rooted weed and wiped petulantly at her face, unaware that she left a broad streak of dirt on her cheek, when a voice behind her said, "Whatever are you doing on your knees in the dirt?"

For a moment Emily wanted to run away, but then her anger took over and she struggled to her feet and turned to face the viscount. "I am gardening," she said defiantly.

His black eyes slid over her and she grew aware that her gown was stained, her hair awry, and her hands covered with dirt. The knowledge brought the blood to her cheeks.

"So I see," returned his lordship. "But is it necessary to go at it so violently? That gown appears to be ruined, you have dirtied your face, and look at your hands."

"I don't care!" Emily could contain her rage no longer. Quite fortunately the house was built like most London town houses, so that the courtyard was surrounded by the house and therefore quite private. But even if it had not been, she could not have waited. "You have treated me abominably," she cried, not caring if the servants heard her. "How dare you forbid me the use of the carriage?"

The viscount viewed her nonchalantly, as though he were faced with raging women every day. "I did not forbid you the use of the carriage."

"You did! You did! And you didn't even have the decency to tell me. You let me find out from the servants."

Her breast heaved under the thin muslin gown and she clenched her dirtied hands into fists. "You have treated me abominably."

"Really, Miss Penthorne," he began in that laconic rake's tone.

Then Emily lost all sense of judgment and launched herself at him, doubled fists striking at his waistcoat. Since that article was buff striped with yellow, the assault of dirtied fists was immediately recorded.

For a moment his lordship stood in stunned surprise and then, when she showed no signs of stopping, and indeed continued the attack with renewed vigor, he attempted to expostulate with her. "Miss Penthorne, stop this. Stop this instantly."

His words, however, had no effect and finally he grabbed her violently by the shoulders. "Emily! Stop!" He shook her harshly till her curls bounced. "Stop this instant."

All the strength went out of her then, all the pent-up rage seemed gone, and she went so limp in his hands that he was forced to draw her against him to support her. There, her cheek against his dirtied waistcoat, she burst into tears.

Now she had disgraced herself even further. How could she convince him that she was a woman when she kept acting like a little girl? There against his waistcoat, she sobbed out her frustration. He simply stood and held her.

Finally the tears ceased. Emily felt completely emptied. There was no rage inside her now—only a terrible void. With his heart beating under her ear, she admitted the truth. She would never, never love anyone but Dunstan. As long as he refused to return that love, she would have to live with this gnawing emptiness inside her.

Finally he put her from him, took a cambric handkerchief from his pocket, and wiped her face.

With his arm still around her, he led her toward a small stone bench and seated her there.

"I am truly sorry to have caused you so much grief," he said in a very gentle tone. "I had intended to tell you about the carriage myself. But I was called away on some business. I do not forbid you the use of the carriage. I merely want to know ahead of time where you plan to go and with whom."

"But why?" Emily felt a small resurgence of anger.

"I want to protect you," he said. "The city is still rather new to you. You might plan to do something dangerous without being aware of it."

"I only wanted to go shopping on Bond Street. And I meant to take Sarah. I mostly wanted to look. I would not exceed my allowance."

The viscount nodded gravely. "I know that. But please believe me, this measure is for your own safety."

Emily forced herself to nod. She supposed he believed what he said and perhaps he could not understand how humiliated it made her feel.

"Good." He smiled at her warmly. "Now you are behaving like a sensible girl."

The anger that Emily had thought dissipated suddenly reared its ugly head, given new strength by that detested word—girl.

She sprang to her feet and drew herself erect.

94

"I am a woman," she said, her tone daring him to deny it. "And I wish to be treated like one."

The viscount's features hardened and he too got to his feet. "In that case you must begin acting like one." Raking her over once more with eyes like glowing black coals, he turned on his heels and strode away.

Once more Emily sank back on the bench and gave way to tears. For a moment she had felt really close to him, and then he had spoiled it all. With that one word he had spoiled it all. Would he never cease regarding her as a spoiled little girl?

## CHAPTER 8

The days passed as days do. They saw Kean play
Iago, a pleasure vaguely disconcerting to Emily,
who could not banish the picture of his Othello.
They went to Covent Garden to see the great
Kemble play Macbeth, which he did with con-
summate style. On both these occasions they were
accompanied by Lord Bersford and Sarah. Emily,
watching her friend's happiness grow, could only
hope that this time there would be no heartbreak
to follow.

She herself could not get into the spirit of the
coming Victory Celebration. She had managed to
avoid meeting the eye of Lord Gilcrest on both
occasions at the theater. She had dressed in a
manner the viscount would approve. She had

learned gracefully to ask for the carriage in advance (and true to his word Dunstan always let her have it); but she had not succeeded in getting him to treat her differently.

He was invariably polite and kind. Sometimes Emily almost wished for a quarrel. It might be worth being yelled at if she could end up in his arms as she had that day in the garden. But, since there was no way of insuring such a good outcome, she decided it was wiser to forego such action.

May moved into June and all of London was agog over the expected visit of the Emperor of Russia and the King of Prussia, England's allies in the great struggle against Napoleon.

One morning Sarah picked up the *Morning Chronicle* and announced, "They're here." She began to read: "His Imperial Majesty, Alexander of Russia, his Prussian Majesty, and the illustrious princes and princesses in their respective suites, arrived yesterday in London, at different hours, and by different routes, to avoid the *éclat* of a public entry, and, consequently, to avoid the pressure of the multitudes who had assembled to welcome their approach." She paused and scanned the page, then continued. "The Emperor of Russia arrived at half-past two o'clock, at the Pulteney Hotel, in so private a manner that the post boys did not know who they were driving. He traveled in Count Lieven's carriage without a single attendant; he passed all the attendants in the lower part of the Hotel without his being known, and had run up to the first flight of stairs, when Prince Gargarine announced that it was the emperor. At the same instant his sister, the Grand Duchess, met him on the stairs, and they saluted each other in the most affectionate manner. The Emperor afterwards embraced the interesting child, Prince Alexander."

As Sarah paused, Emily asked idly, "Has the emperor no wife?"

"He has one," replied Sarah. "The Princess Elizabeth of Baden. He did not bring her along."

Emily looked rather grave and seemed to be debating with herself before she spoke. Apparently she then decided that Emily was of an age to be informed. "They say she is rather delicate." There was a long pause. "The emperor has the reputation of having an eye for the ladies. He is quite a handsome man, they say—tall and lean, with fair hair and deep blue eyes."

Emily shrugged. "Well, that explains leaving the princess behind. He wouldn't want to be hampered by a wife."

Sarah frowned. "Emily, you are becoming quite cynical, not at all like your old cheerful self. The emperor is here on state business, not for pleasure."

Emily contented herself with a nod. She would not bother to contradict Sarah, but she was rather sure that the emperor, being a man, would not turn down any chances he might encounter. Since he was an emperor and attractive, there was no doubt that chances would abound.

Perhaps even Harriette Wilson . . . Unaware, Emily frowned. Harriette Wilson was often on her mind these days, especially when his lordship dined away from home. She could not forget the look those two had exchanged that night at Drury Lane. Certainly his lordship went somewhere in the evenings, many evenings. He had said that he did not game heavily, so why would he spend that much time at White's?

Emily sighed. She had fought and fought with herself over her partiality for Dunstan. It was ridiculous, the worst kind of folly. She told herself so repeatedly, but none of that did any good. She had even cast her eyes around surreptitiously at the theater and other places they had been, to see if there might not be somebody who could take her mind off the man who persisted in seeing her as a child. But beside him, every other man seemed insignificant.

"Emily." Sarah's voice sounded annoyed and Emily realized that she had not been listening.

"Yes, Sarah?"

"I said, I should like to see the emperor. Perhaps we can find a place in a building and see him go by. It says here: 'The joyful tidings of the arrival of the emperor resounded, not only throughout the house, but in the street, where there was an immense concourse of people, who expressed their joy by repeated huzzahs and "Long live the emperor," etc., etc. He, in consequence, appeared, a short time afterwards, at the balcony, and bowed in the most condescending manner, which he continued to do at intervals, till eleven o'clock at night, the people rending the air with shouts of applause.'"

Emily considered this. It might be interesting to see the emperor. It might be something to do to relieve the ennui she sometimes felt. Bond Street's shops held no more allure for her and sometimes she was driven by a terrible need to do something exciting. The problem was that she did not know what. "What else does it say?"

"They are fitting up a bed for him in St. James's Palace, a new state bed of crimson velvet with gold lace and fringe, a crown at the top, and appropriate ornaments."

Emily smiled. "The emperor should look quite well in such luxury."

Sarah did not smile. "Do you suppose we could go to see them pass?"

"I don't see why not. I shall ask his lordship for the carriage. And why don't you ask Bersford to accompany us?"

Sarah's face glowed at this thought and Emily sighed again, wishing that she were, like Sarah, assured of the love of the man she cared for.

At that moment the door opened to admit Dunstan. Emily felt the color rush to her cheeks and bent her attention on her teacup till the color faded.

"Good morning," said the viscount.

"Good morning, milord," echoed Sarah and Emily.

Emily felt Sarah's eyes upon her and so was forced to look up to where his lordship stood. "Sarah and I were just reading the account of the allied sovereigns' arrival."

Dunstan nodded. "I understand the streets were packed."

"Yes. And—well—" Now that the task was upon her, Emily did not find it so easy. "Well, Sarah and I wondered if we might have the carriage and go see the emperor. After all, it isn't often that we get such royal visitors. We might ask Viscount Bersford to accompany us." She paused and realized suddenly that underlying the suggestion that Bersford accompany them, was her wish that Dunstan make up one of the party.

His lordship seemed to be considering, and Emily waited rather anxiously. She did not care much about seeing the emperor; she did care about keeping Dunstan's approval.

Finally he spoke. "If Bersford is available, I approve. I do not wish you to expose yourselves to the crush without having a man along. Unfortunately I am rather busy at this time and will be unable to accompany you myself."

Emily fought to keep her disappointment from showing on her face. Was this business with Harriette Wilson?

"You had best check out the emperor's itinerary. Perhaps Bersford or I know someone with a place along the intended route."

"That would be nice," agreed Sarah. "We may be above the crush and still have a good view."

Dunstan nodded. "An excellent idea. I will speak to Bersford about it directly." He consulted his watch. "In fact, I must be on my way now."

Watching him stride off, so lean and handsome, Emily realized that she had just let out a great sigh of relief. If he was seeing Bersford, then he would not be seeing Harriette Wilson.

A few days later Bersford arrived quite early in the morning to escort them to a house near Whitehall Stairs where the illustrious visitors were to embark for a trip by water to Woolwich.

Emily clutched her handkerchief as Bersford helped them into the carriage. She was glad to be doing something; she looked forward to seeing the visitors.

However, being with Sarah and her Bersford had grown daily more trying. It was not that they excluded Emily from their conversations, though they did that sometimes. It was that in their partiality for each other they were so ecstatic, so glowing.

Emily certainly wished her friend every happiness, and on closer acquaintance she had grown to approve of Bersford. But the sight of their happiness increased the terrible yearning within her, a yearning that could only be silenced by Dunstan's love.

But this day Bersford was busy. He led them up the stairs to the balcony that he had gotten for them. As the two women settled on the chairs he had put there, Emily saw that the street had begun to fill with people. The buildings across the way showed open windows and balconies where ladies waited. She looked toward the river where carved and gilded barges sparkled in the sun. There were certainly enough of them. All the City Companies must have their barges out, as well as those of the Admiralty, the Navy, and the Ordnance Board. Their gay bunting and silken flags provided a festive air. She could also see the launches of the ship *Enterprise;* and from the distance floated the sounds of martial music, produced no doubt by bands aboard some of the boats.

Emily felt a certain sense of excitement as she watched the crowds continue to gather. But when she turned to speak to Sarah, her companion and Bersford were engaged in a quiet conversation. Emily turned back to the street. If Bersford could only persuade his parents to consent, she would soon lose her companion.

Her mind drifted away to thoughts of how pleasant it would be if she and Sarah could be married at the same time. She could see herself at the altar, resplendent in a dress of white satin and Brussels lace, looking up into Dunstan's face, finally able to let him read her devotion for him, his own face reflecting love for her.

Emily sighed. There was no use in having such daydreams. Dunstan never saw her as a woman.

The sounds below grew louder and she looked out in the direction from which the dignitaries were supposed to come. "Look, Sarah, I think that's the emperor coming now."

As the group grew closer, Emily could make out more of the emperor's looks. His uniform of bright green velvet marked him as an important person and the decorations blazing on his chest were embedded with diamonds. As the carriage moved slowly through the packed streets, he bowed graciously this way and that.

Beside him in the carriage sat a woman. It was difficult to see her features, especially as she wore a great straw bonnet shaded by a broad pendant feather, but she held herself quite proudly. Emily had heard that the emperor's sister, Catherine, Duchess of Oldenburgh, was noted for her independence and liveliness of mind, for her sharp tongue and mocking vivacity. She certainly held herself as though she thought she was of high value. She, too, bowed graciously toward the clamoring throng.

Emily rose from her chair and leaned over the balcony to get a better look. Was the emperor really as handsome as everyone said? she wondered. As her hand closed over the railing, it met something wet and slick and she felt the handkerchief slip from her fingers.

At that precise instant the emperor's carriage passed beneath her and the white cambric square edged with lace floated down right into the hand with which he was saluting the populace. Emily stood rooted to the spot as Alexander stopped the carriage and regarded the slip of material in his hand. Then he turned his eyes up toward the balcony where Emily still stood. Even from that distance she could feel the heat of his eyes as he surveyed her. She knew she should move away from the railing, but somehow she was paralyzed. She simply stood there as Alexander's gaze held hers for some moments. Then he raised his hand in a gay salute and ordered the carriage on.

Emily did not return his salute and indeed it was some moments before the paralysis left her limbs. She noticed that he turned to one of the dignitaries that rode beside him, as though asking a question. Then she grew conscious that Sarah was beside her. "Emily! Emily! You must come sit down."

Silently Emily allowed herself to be led back to the chair. She was only now realizing what a horrendous thing she had done in calling the czar's attention to herself. If Dunstan heard of this . . . She shivered. He would surely never believe that the handkerchief had slipped from her fingers accidentally. Nor would anyone else in the *ton*.

She began to laugh hysterically. How could she have ever planned something so well? To make a handkerchief fall right into the czar's outstretched hand? No one could do that. Yet everyone would believe that she had.

"Emily." Sarah was looking at her anxiously. "Emily, whatever is wrong with you?"

Emily shook her head, her laughter turning to hysterical sobs. "Nothing, Sarah, nothing at all. Haven't I just succeeded in getting the Emperor of Russia's attention? Won't that make Dunstan happy?"

She continued to sob until Sarah thrust her own handkerchief into her hand and said sternly, "Emily Penthorne, stop that this minute."

"Now," said Bersford as Emily's sobs quieted. "I must get the two of you home."

Emily turned woeful eyes to him. "Please, please, don't tell Dunstan what happened. It was not my fault, truly it wasn't. The handkerchief slipped. He will be so angry with me, so angry."

Tears stood out in her eyes as Bersford looked

down on her. "I'm sorry, Miss Emily, but I don't see how I can possibly keep it from him. Someone will spread the word. After all, there are many people around here, many members of the *ton.* Everyone will whisper about the woman that the emperor stopped to salute."

"Dear God," wailed a distraught Emily. "He will never let me out now. Oh, what shall I do?"

Sarah patted her charge on the shoulder. "Come dear, you are making too much of this. The viscount is a reasonable man, isn't he, Bersford?"

Sarah's friend nodded, but even to Emily's tear-blurred vision it was apparent that he didn't think the viscount's reaction was going to be good.

"Come, we must be getting back. The crush below has dissipated somewhat. We will go down the stairs to the alley in back. We should be able to get out that way."

"Come, Emily," said Sarah. "Dry your eyes now and come along."

"Yes, Sarah." Emily managed to stifle the tears, but she could not stop the ache in her heart. He was going to find her conduct indefensible and she knew it.

Dunstan was not in the house on St. James's Square when the little group arrived there. Emily went straight to her room to wash her tear-streaked face and to compose herself. But, as she sat in the light of the window with her needlework, she could not concentrate on it. She knew he was going to be angry. Her mind was so absorbed with the coming disaster that she pricked herself sharply with the needle and muttered a small oath. The worst of it was that it was so unfair. She hadn't the least desire in the world to be noticed by some woman-chasing emperor. She only wanted to be noticed by Dunstan.

It was half an hour later when the knock sounded on the door. "Yes?" called Emily, her heart in her mouth.

"It's me, miss," said Jeffers, opening the door slightly.

"Yes, Jeffers."

"His lordship is just home, miss." Jeffers looked more than a little uncomfortable. "And he wishes to see you in the library, miss. Now." The way in which the footman pronounced that last word was all the indication Emily needed. Dunstan was certainly very angry.

"I'm going right away," she said. "Thank you." She dropped the needlework and was out the door.

She almost tripped on the stairs in her haste not to keep him waiting, but by the time she had reached the library she slowed her steps. The whole thing was so miserably unfair. Well, she told herself, she would just keep calm and tell him the truth, that it was not her fault.

She stepped through the library door. "Milord?"

He turned from where he was looking out the

window and scowled at her. She had seen him angry, but never this enraged. "Come in, Miss Penthorne. We have a matter to discuss."

Emily advanced on trembling legs. "Yes, milord?"

"Please be seated." The viscount indicated a chair and Emily sank into it, grateful for the support.

"I think that I have been fulfilling my duties as guardian adequately," he began. "I think that I have not refused you the carriage for any reasonable request. Is that correct?"

"Yes, milord." Emily forced herself to sit up straight and look undismayed.

"I think that I have bent over backward to be amenable to your wants. And now, now you have rewarded me with the most reprehensible behavior."

"To what behavior do you allude?" asked Emily, speaking in her grandest manner in order to hide the fear she felt.

"To your behavior near Whitehall Stairs this morning," he replied curtly. "To behave in such a hoydenish fashion." He shook his head. "I cannot believe it."

"I did not do anything," asserted Emily, quite aware that she was not convincing him.

"Not do anything!" he cried. "You dropped your handkerchief into the hand of the Emperor of Russia. He stopped his carriage to salute you and learn your identity. And you say you did nothing."

"I did not drop my handkerchief on purpose," Emily replied, determined not to cry. "It fell from my hand."

"Most conveniently when Alexander was passing below." Dunstan look at her in disbelief.

"Can't you see?" cried the distraught Emily. "No one could drop a handkerchief so purposely like that and have it land so well. It was pure chance. The railing was wet and slippery and the handkerchief fell from my fingers. That was all."

From the look on his lordship's face it was quite apparent that he did not believe her. "Certainly you were not unaware of the emperor's penchant for an attractive woman."

Emily's heart leaped momentarily at the word woman.

"Surely you must expect him to want to discover the identity of the one who had so brazenly brought herself to his attention?"

"I did not bring myself to his attention," insisted Emily, a spark of anger in her igniting at his obstinance. "Why will you not believe what I say? The handkerchief fell from my hand."

' "And you stood there, returning his look, until he moved on. If it was all an accident, why didn't you retreat from his sight?"

"I couldn't." Emily paused. This explanation was not going well at all. "My legs would not work. I was so startled and surprised by what had happened."

The viscount frowned fiercely. Obviously he did not believe this either. "Emily, Emily, what am I going to do with you? This kind of behavior is extremely dangerous. To quiz me on the London Road, that was bad enough. You were fortunate in the fact that the man was me. But Alexander . . . He has no scruples where women are concerned. Now that he knows your identity, he will seek you out. Then what will you do?"

Emily straightened her shoulders even further. "I am quite capable of taking care of myself," she said stiffly. "I shall just tell Alexander that the whole thing was a mistake. He should have sense enough to believe me."

The viscount laughed harshly, the sound grating on her ears. "You are trying to fool me. No man of Alexander's stature—and looks—would believe such a thing. Why, every woman in the *ton* is eager to get close to him."

"Certainly I cannot help that," replied Emily stiffly. "I am not responsible for the actions of the *ton.*"

Dunstan eyed her strangely. "You say that you can take care of yourself, but I do not believe it. You are young and innocent. I hope! " He glared at her again. "I warn you, have a care how you behave. This is more important than you think."

Emily sighed. "I am grateful for your concern,"

she said in a voice utterly devoid of gratitude. "But it would be much more acceptable if you had some faith in me. I am not the silly girl you believe me to be." She drew herself up to her full height. "What happened this morning was an accident—pure and simple. I did nothing wrong. I do not believe an apology is in order. Therefore if you are quite finished, I should like to go to my room for a while. This whole thing has been rather disturbing to me."

She blinked rapidly to keep back the rising tears. How utterly stupid it was to want to throw herself against his waistcoat and plead for forgiveness.

The viscount returned her look gravely and then shook his head. "I have done all that I can," he said solemnly. "The rest is up to you."

"Then," replied Emily with great dignity, "I assure you that I am quite safe." With that she turned on her heels and left the room. No longer daring to stay in his presence, she sought the sanctuary of her chamber, where she threw herself onto the bed and sobbed out her anger and her anguish. She loved him. She loved him madly. And the Viscount Dunstan still saw her only as a spoiled, ungrateful chit.

# CHAPTER 9

The next several days Emily stayed indoors. She did not want to risk being anywhere near Alexander. In spite of her brave words to Dunstan about being able to care for herself, she was not certain as to how she would handle a meeting with the emperor.

But finally she grew extremely bored and restless, and one evening she approached the viscount with a request for permission to use the carriage to go to Bond Street the following day. After a rather hard look, he granted it.

When Sarah and Emily were on their way to go shopping, Sarah shook her head. "I do not understand you, Emily. First you refuse to leave the house and now you insist on shopping."

Emily shrugged. "I do not understand myself, Sarah. I only know that I must be doing something." She paused. "I think we'll go to the *modiste*. I need a new gown for Lady Cholmondoley's ball, and I have not yet replaced the one that Dunstan sent back."

Sarah sighed. "Just be circumspect about it, will you?"

Emily smiled. "Of course I will. I don't like to have scenes with the viscount. They just happen."

Sarah nodded soberly. "I know, dear. Well, we shall do the best we can. What color do you have in mind?"

"Perhaps something in celestial blue," Emily replied, thinking of how his lordship had said blue was becoming to her.

"You do have a lot of blue," began Sarah, but at that moment the carriage drew up before Madame Ferre's establishment.

Emily sprang out quickly and stood waiting for Sarah. Another carriage waited in the street, an open carriage. As she passed it, Emily gasped. "Look, Sarah, it's lined in blue satin."

Sarah frowned. "I have heard that such a carriage belongs to Harriette Wilson. We had best get back in our own and move on."

Emily did not turn back. "Nonsense, Sarah. I merely want to order a new gown. I cannot help it if someone else is there." Without waiting further, Emily continued into the shop. There was nothing for Sarah to do but follow.

As Emily entered she looked quickly around. A few nondescript women were examining material. A young shop girl fluttered quickly to the fore and greeted them.

"I wish to order a new gown," said Emily.

"Yes, miss. If you'll just look around a little, Madame Ferre is busy with another customer. She'll be with you shortly."

"Very well," said Emily. "I will wait." She busied herself with examining the various bolts of material around the room. She especially liked a pale-blue satin and was rubbing it gently between her thumb and fingers as Sarah stood by when the door to the inner chamber opened.

Emily knew she should not stare. Indeed, she knew she should turn her back to the beautiful Harriette Wilson. But she did not. She ignored Sarah's pulling at her arm. Here was her chance to see what Harriette Wilson looked like—the Harriette Wilson that she suspected was the cause of Dunstan spending so many evenings away from the house on St. James's Square.

She found herself looking up just as the celebrated demi-rep passed. Her gown was of coral-sprigged muslin and she wore no jewels. Her rich auburn hair tumbled in the fashionable style and a poke bonnet swung from her gloved hand. Then, suddenly, Emily found herself meeting the infamous woman's eyes. They held a certain merriment and, as Harriette smiled and inclined her head slightly, Emily did the same.

She heard Sarah's quick indrawn breath, but she continued to watch as the Queen of Hearts passed out of the shop, saying to Madame Ferre, who hovered at her heels like an anxious puppy, "I shall expect the gowns Tuesday next then."

"*Oui, mademoiselle.* They shall come." The *modiste* clasped her hands. "You will like. I am certain."

Then the incognita was gone and Emily looked back to the blue satin in her hand. What had that look in Harriette's eyes meant? And why had she nodded as she had?

"*Mademoiselle,*" repeated the anxious little *modiste*. "You like your gowns? You do not return more?"

Emily, her thoughts pulled back to the present, nodded. "I like the gowns I ordered. The return of the blue muslin was not my wish. My—guardian did not approve it."

Now why, thought Emily, had she paused like that before the word guardian, as though she wanted to say something else?

The *modiste* nodded. "The viscount, he was right. I should not have sold you such a gown. It was—was—*impudique*—immodest. I apologize to the viscount. He say he understand."

118

In spite of the viscount's understanding, Madame Ferre looked anxious. Emily hastened to reassure her. "It's all right, madame. The other gowns were quite beautiful. I wish to order a new one—for Lady Cholmondoley's ball."

"*Oui, oui.* You like this blue satin?" The *modiste* looked down at the bolt before them.

Emily considered it. "Yes, show me some patterns. Something that the viscount would approve."

"*Oui, oui, mademoiselle.* You will come sit down?"

"Yes."

Emily trailed along behind Madame Ferre into the private chamber where she gave all her attentions to the patterns Madame solicitously displayed before her.

Sarah, too, was called in for consultation. "I do like this silk," she said, but it was obvious that her attention was elsewhere. The meeting with Harriette Wilson had disturbed her.

"Come, Sarah," said Emily. "Do not go woolgathering now. This gown must be beautiful—and correct."

Sarah nodded and seemed to make an effort to concentrate on the task at hand.

"I like this neckline," she said, and Emily agreed. It was certainly high enough to meet the viscount's approval, yet it would show her throat nicely.

"And I believe the little sleeves with self-ruching. And the same around the neck. Don't you think so, Sarah?"

Her companion agreed. "And several rows around the skirt, say three or four."

Madame nodded enthusiastically. "*Bon, bon.* That is the very thing. Mademoiselle will be *parfaite, très belle.* All eyes will be upon her."

Emily felt the color flooding her cheeks. "We must be sure, madame. The viscount must approve this gown."

Madame Ferre nodded vigorously. "He will approve. This I know. *Certainement.* The gown— the other gown he brought back to me himself. He explain what is correct for Mademoiselle. This will be most fine. *Magnifique.*"

Emily felt a little twinge of elation. Had he cared so much that he had visited the *modiste* himself? Then suspicion raised its ugly head. She had seen Harriette Wilson in this shop. Perhaps Dunstan's acquaintance with Madame Ferre's establishment had begun long before Emily Penthorne became one of her customers.

"Emily." Emily grew aware that Sarah was repeating her name.

"Yes, Sarah. I'm listening."

"I believe your blue kid slippers will go with this gown."

Emily nodded and turned to Madame Ferre. "You will have it ready before Lady Cholmondoley's ball, won't you?"

"*Oui, oui. Mademoiselle* is not to worry. It will be delivered on time. Mademoiselle will be—how you say it—belle of the ball."

Emily and Sarah rose. "I believe that is all for today," said Emily.

Madame Ferre followed them obsequiously to the door. "Mademoiselle Penthorne, I am honor that you patronize my establishment. You will come again when you need the most beautiful gown?"

"Yes. Thank you, Madame Ferre. Good day."

"*Au revoir.*"

As the shop door closed behind them, Sarah sighed deeply. Emily turned to her. "Sarah, you do think the gown is all right?"

Her companion nodded. "The gown will be lovely, just as Madame said. It is your meeting with Harriette Wilson that I am concerned about."

As they climbed into the carriage, Emily sighed. "She looked right at me. I could not cut her dead. I just couldn't."

"We shouldn't have gone in when we knew she was there. The viscount will be displeased."

"The viscount? You won't tell him about this, will you?"

Sarah frowned. "I won't have to."

"You think Madame Ferre will tell him? Or—" Her heart fell. "Harriette Wilson?"

Sarah shook her head. "It would not be to Madame's benefit. Nor to Harriette Wilson's. You have forgotten that several other ladies were present in the shop."

"I noticed a few women. I did not know them."

"Well, I did. One of them is a bosom-bow of Princess Lieven. And Madame Ferre spoke your name quite clearly. Another I also recognized. She is one of London's busiest gossips." Sarah's frown deepened. "By now Lady Oxston will have called on at least two of her gossips."

"Already?" replied Emily. "We have barely left the shop."

"That matters little," said Sarah. "Lady Oxston will have chosen the two closest."

"But surely no one will bother to tell Dunstan. Just because I didn't give her the cut directly?"

"Emily, Emily, you know so little of the *ton*. The word of your meeting will be all over London before nightfall. The ladies of the *ton* will not speak well of it. Your conquest of Alexander put many of them in a pet. They will be pleased to be scandalized by your exchange of friendly greetings with a demi-rep."

Emily turned angry eyes to her friend. "This is absolutely ridiculous. Just because I did not insult a woman who has done me no harm."

"Emily, Emily, you must not expect the *ton* to be sensible. Those ladies that censure your conduct with Alexander and who frown on your recognition of a demi-rep may well behave with impropriety in secret. But enough of this. The

122

ladies of the *ton* are not our concern. The viscount is."

Emily frowned. "Sarah, what shall I do?"

Sarah shook her head. "I don't know, Emily. I just don't know. The whole thing was most unfortunate."

By this time the carriage had arrived at St. James's Square and Emily dismounted. She was silent as she and Sarah made their way up the walk to the house. There must be something she could do. It was terrible to sit around waiting for Dunstan to descend on her in his wrath.

As she entered the front door, she thought of it. She would tell him herself, give him all the facts. Surely then he would understand. She turned to Parks. "When his lordship returns, please let me know. I wish to speak to him."

"His lordship is in the library," said Parks. "He returned this past hour."

"Good," said Emily, as she untied her bonnet and put it into Sarah's hands. "I shall see him right away." Ignoring Sarah's warning look, she marched off toward the library. Her heart was pounding in her throat by the time she reached it, but she did not pause. She would make him understand.

She took a deep breath and walked in. He was standing by the window that looked out into the street and again she was struck by the breadth of his shoulders. "Milord?"

He turned to face her, a smile creasing his face. "Miss Penthorne, you are looking well today."

"Thank you, milord. I—I have come to speak to you about something."

"Yes? Come and sit down. There is no need to be so formal."

As the viscount showed her to a chair, Emily's anxiety lessened somewhat. He would understand. "I went today to Madame Ferre's to order a gown for Lady Cholmondoley's ball."

"I hope it will be blue," he said pleasantly.

"It will be, milord. And Madame assured me that you will like it."

He nodded. "Yes, Madame and I have come to an agreement about your gowns. That is fine." He eyed her closely. "But that is not what you wanted to speak to me about."

"No, milord, it isn't." She took a deep breath. "At Madame Ferre's—there was someone else there."

"Who else?"

"H-Harriette Wilson." She waited, but he said nothing for a moment.

Then he replied. "You recognized her from the theater." His voice had sobered, but he did not seem angry.

Emily nodded. "She was ordering a gown."

He continued to listen.

124

"And—and when she walked out, she nodded to me."

He still remained silent.

"And—and I nodded back."

"You what?"

It wasn't going to work. She saw that now. But it was too late.

"She looked right at me. I couldn't—I couldn't cut her dead. I couldn't. She's a friend of yours." Emily was clutching at straws now and she knew it. "Anyway, I didn't think. I just nodded back."

Dunstan got to his feet and began to pace the room. "This is impossible. First you drop your handkerchief into Alexander's outstretched hand, and now you strike up an acquaintance with London's leading incognita."

Emily stood up. She had been foolish to think that he would understand. He understood nothing. He was just an arrogant tyrant. "I did not strike up an acquaintance. I merely nodded."

He turned in his pacing. "I suppose there were others present."

"Yes, Sarah recognized Lady Oxston."

The viscount's face darkened. "London's busiest gossip. She would have to be there. Who else?"

"A bosom-bow of the Princess Lieven."

His lordship muttered a curse. "The princess! Now you've done it up brown!"

"I don't understand."

"The Princess Lieven is an intimate of Alexander's. By now he knows that the beauty he saw the other day has a nodding acquaintance with London's best-known incognita." He glared at her. "Now he will certainly attempt to see you."

"I shall simply be out."

His lordship's frown deepened. "He will not be foolish enough to come calling. He will find some other way, unless I keep you at home until he leaves London."

Emily's anger flared even higher. "You wouldn't!"

His lordship smiled cynically. "You mistake me, my dear. I would—except that the *ton* would certainly talk even more." He resumed his pacing. "No, we must proceed as though nothing has happened. That will cause the least gossip."

By now Emily was too angry to think straight. "I do not understand why my behavior was so terrible," she cried. "What's so wrong with nodding to her anyway? Half of London's ladies are just as bad. They are hypocrites. Little Harry is at least honest."

His lordship came to a halt in front of her. His black eyebrows drawn into a ferocious line, he looked down into her eyes. "Little Harry, is it! The next thing you will be giving me a list of her conquests. I have had enough of this infantile behavior," he said curtly. "Emily, go to your room, and remain there until you have a better sense of what is becoming to a young woman."

For a moment Emily was struck speechless. Sent to her room like a naughty child!

What control she had left deserted her, and she struck out at him with her fists. "I won't! I won't be treated like a bad little girl!"

This time, however, his lordship moved quickly and pulled her into his arms. As she came to a halt against his waistcoat, Emily's anger grew stronger and she struggled fiercely to free herself. But it was no use. He held her so tightly that she could not escape and finally her struggles ceased.

"You must learn to control yourself, Emily. Such behavior is very unladylike. We shall never find you a husband at this rate."

"I don't want a husband," said Emily against his chest. It was only partly a lie—she did not want any husband but him.

He put her from him. "We will not discuss marriage now. I know that things are different in Essex, but this is London. You must learn to behave more circumspectly. Go upstairs now."

She stiffened.

"Just to refresh yourself. I am not punishing you." He sighed and passed a hand over his unruly black hair. "I am ill-equipped for the task of guardian. I have had too little experience with young women of your kind."

She had no answer to this, but turned and made her way out the door. No matter what she did, she could not please him. What was she to do when men started making offers for her? She could not turn them down forever. More important, she certainly could not tell her guardian that she refused to consider anyone else because she had conceived a partiality for him.

## CHAPTER 10

The next several days passed and Emily did not go shopping again. Then a footman came with a message from the patronesses of Almack's. His lordship was at home and Emily took it to him immediately. "Look, this has come from the ladies at Almack's."

"Have you opened it yet?"

Emily shook her head. "I—I am afraid."

Dunstan laughed. "Afraid? You?"

Emily did not take umbrage at this. "Last season I waited all year and I never got to Almack's."

The viscount took the message from her trembling fingers and broke the seal. He held up the coveted vouchers. "It appears that we are going to Almack's."

"Oh!" Emily could not forbear a little skip of joy. "We are going to Almack's. Oh, I shall have to choose a gown."

"I hope it will be blue," he said.

"Yes, yes," cried Emily. "Oh, it's only three days away." With another little skip she was off to tell Sarah the wonderful news.

Tuesday came quite soon and Emily, as she descended the stairs in her gown of deep blue, felt her heart pounding in her throat. Around that throat hung the single strand of pearls—the pearls the viscount had told her to wear before.

The viscount stood at the foot of the stairs, resplendent in knee breeches, white cravat, and chapeau bras. She paused as she reached him and looked up into his face. There was something in his eyes that reminded her of their first meeting and she reddened.

"You are quite lovely tonight," he said. His eyes lingered at her throat. "Your choice of jewels was wise."

"Th-thank you, milord," Emily replied.

Then Sarah appeared and they were off. As the carriage hurried up the street, Emily looked out the window. "Gracious, it's almost as crowded as Drury Lane."

His lordship nodded. "Yes, Almack's is very popular. All the mamas want to display their daughters. It's really a marriage mart. Your voucher gives you the chance to be surveyed by prospective husbands."

Emily frowned. "Ugh! How mercenary. Like being on display in a shop window."

His lordship shrugged. "That is the way it is done." He looked out his window. "The crush will be worse later. I have come early on purpose so as not to risk being turned away. Old Willis is adamant about the hours the ladies have agreed on."

"I hope I shall be able to remember the steps to the waltz," said Emily nervously. "I have not practiced for some time."

"I shall lead you out myself," said the viscount. "There is really nothing to fear. You just lean back on my hand and follow."

"Yes, milord," said Emily, wondering what he would say if he knew that just the prospect of being in his arms made her pulses pound.

Finally the carriage approached the door and Dunstan helped Emily and Sarah out and escorted them up the stairs. As they entered the ballroom, Emily felt his lordship's grip on her elbow tighten and heard him mutter something indistinguishable.

"Milord?" she inquired, but he shook his head and did not repeat himself.

Emily saw that the ballroom was rather large and barren. Along one wall was arranged a row of chairs and upon the chairs were enthroned a num-

ber of stout dowagers. None of them was dressed
with much *élan,* thought Emily, eyeing their gowns
with distaste. One woman looked particularly
shocking. She was wearing green-and-white
striped silk that would surely have been more
suitable on a sofa. Over her unusually jet black
curls towered an enormous orange ostrich plume.
It swayed dangrously as she leaned toward her
neighbor.

"Who is that in the green-and-white silk?" Emily
asked Dunstan, receiving a frown in reply.

"Lady Oxston. Mark my word, she will see everything you do—and some things you don't. So have
a care."

"I shall," replied Emily, now recognizing in
this flamboyant peacock one of the nondescript
ladies at Madame Ferre's.

She looked around her. The ballroom was perhaps half full and more guests were arriving every
moment. Emily became engrossed in examining
the gowns of the women. It was clear that some
ladies had damped their petticoats, and that some
of them were not particularly young ladies. Emily
felt the color rise to her cheeks as one young
woman passed. She was wearing a gown that
could have been the twin of the one Dunstan had
insisted on returning. The way it clung left no
doubt that her petticoat, and a light one, too, had
been liberally damped. Emily, turning to the viscount to admit the correctness of his decision,

found that his eyes were following the young woman with attention.

The words of apology died in her throat as terrible waves of jealousy swept over her. So! She could not wear anything so brazen, but he could admire it on other women. She turned away and with great effort restrained herself. She would show him! She would just show him that men could find her attractive too, and without her brazenly displaying herself like a common lightskirt.

She let her eyes rove over the room. What she needed was the attention of another man, someone who could make the viscount jealous. If only that were possible, she thought with a sigh.

Then her eyes were caught and held by those of a tall, fair man with a sharp face. Lord Gilcrest smiled and Emily inclined her head the barest minimum.

She turned immediately to Sarah and his lordship, who were busily engaged in a conversation about Bersford's future, and pretended to be immensely interested. How Dunstan would rage if he discovered that she had countenanced Gilcrest's smile. Fortunately, he need never know.

"Ah, Dunstan." Gilcrest's hearty accents caused the three of them to turn. "I see our charmer here has earned the right to enter the sacred portals."

"It appears so," said the viscount dryly.

Gilcrest turned to Emily. "May I say, Miss

133

Penthorne, that I am pleased beyond measure to see you here. You have made my evening complete." He bent low over her gloved hand.

"You are too kind, milord," she replied. Her eyes were caught by his as he raised his head and something in them caused her to shiver. There was a look there, as of a predatory beast, she thought. But then the look was gone and Gilcrest was all genial affability.

His fingers still held hers, and when Emily sought to withdraw her hand, his grip tightened. "I must ask you for the favor of the next waltz," he said urbanely.

Emily's breath quickened. One glance at Dunstan told her clearly that he was quite angry. His features remained serene, but a telltale muscle in his jaw quivered.

Emily smiled ruefully. "I am sorry, milord, but I have promised my first waltz to my guardian."

Gilcrest frowned momentarily, but quickly rallied. "Then I shall return later." He turned to his lordship. "I must say, Dunstan, that this is deuced unfair. You have this gem at hand all the time while the rest of us—" He smiled again at Emily. "Until later," he said and then went to seek another partner.

Emily looked to his lordship. The muscle in his jaw had ceased quivering, but he did not smile at her or offer a compliment. Instead, he frowned. "I do not like that man. He is a fortune hunter, out for the main chance." He turned to her. "Well, I suppose we must have our waltz now so as not to prove you a prevaricator."

Emily felt the anger rising. He needn't be so condescending about it! After all, he had said he would lead her out.

"If you find waltzing with me too much trouble," she said sharply, "it is quite all right. I'm sure I shall have other partners."

His lordship gave her a surprised glance. "I'm sure you shall, but don't fly up in the boughs on me. I said I would lead you out and I shall." He took her hand and led her to the dance floor.

Emily's fingers were trembling and her knees felt weak. It was not the prospect of dancing that affected her so, but the thought of being in Dunstan's arms.

The strains of the waltz swept through the room and Emily, caught up in his lordship's arms, was swept with them. Round and round the room they whirled. Emily caught only glimpses of the faces around them as they dipped and swirled. She was lost in the glory of being in his arms, of being close to him as she had yearned to be for so long.

The waltz was exhilarating, and when the music drew to an end, she found her irritation with Dunstan had vanished. "That was great fun," she said, smiling up at him.

There was no answering smile on his face.

"You waltz admirably. You need have no further fear." He led her back to Sarah. All Emily's elation fled as swiftly as it had come. He seemed always to be saying the very thing that irritated her.

As they approached her friend, Emily saw that Bersford had arrived. Now, she thought bitterly, she would have no one to talk to. Sarah and Bersford were a world to themselves and Dunstan seemed particularly edgy. That seemed strange to her, for he had certainly been affable enough in the carriage. She sighed. She had so wanted to enjoy this evening. Then she straightened her shoulders. Well, she would enjoy it. Let his lordship be out of sorts if he chose, she did not have to be affected by it.

Almost as though her thoughts had been heard, a gentleman approached and asked her to join him in a quadrille. She accepted gladly, determined to join the dancing and have fun.

She did enjoy herself, but when she returned at the close of several sets, she found Dunstan gone. "Where is his lordship?" she asked Sarah.

Sarah paused in her conversation with Bersford. "He said he was going to find a lady."

"A lady!" Emily tried to compose her features. "Do you know who she is?"

Sarah shook her head. "No, Emily, I don't."

*A lady,* thought Emily with a frown. *What did Dunstan want with a lady?*

"My dear." Gilcrest's hearty tones burst into her thoughts. "I believe this is our waltz."

Emily gave him her best smile. "I believe so, milord." Putting her hand in his, she followed him to the floor.

It was quite different being in Gilcrest's arms. For one thing, he seemed to hold her very tightly, in a way Emily found rather embarrassing. She tried to pull back a little, but he chuckled. "Do not be frightened, my dove. You must give yourself into my power."

As Emily raised startled eyes to his, he smiled the cynical smile of the rake. "For the dance, of course. It is the only way to succeed."

Emily nodded, but somewhere deep inside her something trembled. This man was evil; Dunstan had been right about that. Still, she had agreed to dance with him and surely nothing could happen to her on the dance floor. She gave herself up to the intoxicating rhythm of the waltz.

When the music ended, she found that they were the length of the ballroom from Sarah. "I should very much like to come some afternoon and take you for a drive in Hyde Park," said Gilcrest, still keeping hold of her hand.

"I'm afraid that would be impossible, milord," she said politely. "Lord Dunstan permits me to ride out only with him."

A flash of anger appeared on Gilcrest's face and

was quickly gone. "Of course. How very wise of him. You will excuse me."

Emily was slightly disconcerted to find herself suddenly alone, but she merely shrugged and began to make her way toward Sarah.

She was perhaps halfway across the space between them when she saw Dunstan. He was talking to a girl, the girl in the clinging blue gown. Sharp tears stung at Emily's eyes and she stumbled. A strong hand went immediately under her elbow to help her maintain her balance.

"Thank you," she said and turned to find herself looking into the bright blue eyes of Alexander, Emperor of Russia!

"Miss Penthorne," he said. "I have been waiting to make your acquaintance." He smiled. "In a more formal manner than was possible the other day."

Emily felt the color flood her cheeks. "I—the other day—that was an accident."

"Of course." Alexander bowed urbanely. "But such a fortuitous accident should not be overlooked."

His eyes traveled over her and Emily knew that Dunstan's estimation of the man had been correct.

"You are even lovelier at this close range," he said, his heavily accented voice making the words extremely personal.

138

"I—thank you, your majesty." Emily was at a loss for words. She knew she should move away, but the czar's fingers still held her elbow.

"You will give me the pleasure of the next waltz, will you not, Miss Emily Penthorne?" He smiled at her warmly and Emily was aware of the man's charm.

She was about to refuse him when her mind again presented her with a picture of Dunstan with that girl in the blue gown. "I should be delighted, your majesty." Emily allowed herself to be led onto the floor.

As they swept round and round the room, she kept a bright smile on her face. If anyone was watching—Dunstan in particular—she wanted him to see that she was enjoying herself. If he could talk with that brazen creature, then assuredly there was no harm in her accepting a waltz with Alexander.

"You are very good," he said as the music ended. "I have been much intrigued by our meeting the other day. Much intrigued." His blue eyes held an invitation, and for one wild moment Emily wanted to respond to it. That would show Dunstan!

But common sense came to the fore. "I assure you, your highness, the other day was a complete accident. I was very embarrassed by it."

His smile told her clearly that he did not believe a word she said. "Yes," he repeated. "I am much intrigued. I should like to see you privately, away from all this noise."

"Your highness!" Emily's indignation was not feigned. She found this proposition insulting to the highest degree. "My guardian would never consent to such a thing!"

Alexander smiled wisely. "Of course, my dear. But you may go shopping . . ."

Emily frowned. "I am truly sorry, your highness, that the accident of the other day should have so misled you as to my character. I do not have such meetings as you suggest. They are—improper."

He bowed urbanely. "Of course, of course. I quite understand. But still, I shall be hoping. Perhaps you shall decide to visit Madame Ferre's again, eh? Perhaps I shall be accidentally in the neighborhood."

Emily shook her head in exasperation. What was wrong with men? Could the creatures never believe the truth when it was told them?

"How you spend your mornings is your own concern, your majesty, but if you think to see me on Bond Street, you will be disappointed." Without waiting for further conversation, she made her way toward Sarah.

Surprisingly Sarah and Bersford were not deep in conversation when she approached them. They both turned accusing eyes upon her. *I could not help it,* Emily felt like screaming. *Why must every-one misunderstand me?* "He's the Emperor of Russia. I could not refuse to dance with him."

"And is that all he wanted?" asked Sarah stern-ly.

"Of course it was," lied Emily. "What else could he want?"

Since Sarah was deterred by Bersford's presence from pursuing the subject more specifically, the matter was dropped, but Emily found that her joy in the evening had fled. Dancing with other gentlemen was now a duty she performed, rather than a pleasure she enjoyed.

Even when Dunstan returned to stand beside her, she could not capture her earlier enthusiasm. "You have become strangely quiet," he observed dryly.

Emily sighed. She wanted above all to ask him about that girl, but she dared not. He, in his turn, had certainly seen her with Alexander, and yet he made no comment on the matter. Probably he in-tended to wait until they reached home. Her head began to throb at the thought. "I—I find I have a touch of headache."

"We can leave now if you prefer," he said with alacrity.

Emily sighed deeply. There was no use putting off the inevitable. If they were going to come to cuffs, she might as well get it over with. "Yes, mi-lord, I believe I should. Let us go home now."

They were soon in the carriage and soon at the house in St. James's Square. As they reached the foot of the front stairs, Dunstan turned to Sarah. "I have a little matter to discuss with my ward. Good night, Miss Parker."

"Good night, milord," said Sarah.

As she followed him to the library, Emily tried to compose herself. She had done nothing wrong; she assured herself of that. In fact she had refused two assignations. But she dared not tell him that, or the very fact that they had been offered would enrage him even further.

He shut the door behind them. "Emily, I must speak to you seriously."

"Yes, milord."

"You do not seem to understand my concern for your reputation. Tonight, for instance, you waltzed with Gilcrest—and then Alexander."

"You were not there to dance with me," she defended herself. "All I did was waltz. Surely there is nothing wrong with that."

Dunstan scowled. "The waltz has been known to give men ideas," he said sharply. "It is not wise to encourage a man like Gilcrest."

"I did not encourage him," repeated Emily.

Dunstan ignored this. "And then you waltzed with Alexander, to whom you have never been introduced."

"He knew my name," said Emily and knew instantly that she had made a grave mistake.

"Of course he did! He went to great pains to find it out. And then he got Princess Lieven to issue you a voucher to Almack's so that he could meet you."

Emily stared at him. "But why should he go to all that trouble merely to meet me?"

Dunstan's scowl deepened. "Do not annoy me excessively," he snapped. "It is abundantly clear that Alexander hoped for more than an introduction. The accident of the other day and your apparent friendliness with Harriette Wilson led him to believe that he could get more." He eyed her closely. "I cannot impress upon you enough what dangerous ground you are treading here, Emily. Neither Gilcrest nor Alexander are novices in the petticoat line. When they pursue a woman, they expect to get results. Certain ladies of the *ton* are already convinced that Alexander will continue to meet you privately."

"Certain ladies in blue gowns with damped petticoats no doubt," cried Emily, hardly knowing what she said.

The viscount stared at her. "I am the guardian here," he said stiffly. "I had a matter to discuss with the young lady, but that is no concern of yours. What I wish to impress on you now is the utter stupidity of your consenting to any such meetings."

"Of course, milord," replied Emily far too sweetly. "I understand. You forbid me to meet secretly with Lord Gilcrest or the emperor. Is that all?"

Dunstan frowned. "Do not be deliberately perverse. I am acting in your best interests."

In spite of the fact that she knew he was right, Emily bridled. "I should think that you might give me credit for a modicum of common sense. Just because my handkerchief slipped from my fingers at an inopportune time, you imagine that I am about to embark on an affair with the emperor. And now you suspect me with Gilcrest, too! I am amazed that you do not forbid me the carriage entirely. Certainly that would fit more appropriately your high-handed ways."

Dunstan's face paled and Emily wondered if she had pushed him too far. Well, she told herself defiantly, it was time he learned not to treat her like a child.

For long moments he stared at her, the muscle in his jaw twitching ominously. "I shall not refuse you the carriage," he said finally. "It would be futile. I know you well enough to be sure that carriage or no, if you desired to arrange such a meeting, you would find a way to do so. And, if you were bent on such a foolhardy scheme, you would be safer in the carriage."

"You are too kind, milord," replied Emily caustically. "And now, if you have no more remarks to make on the negative aspects of my character, I shall retire to my bed and leave you to your suspicions."

For another long moment they stared at each other and then Emily turned and marched out. He was infuriating, she thought as she made her way up the stairs. Absolutely infuriating! Here she was, madly in love with him, wanting nothing so much as to belong to him, and all he could do was berate her about other men. As though those others meant anything to her. Why, she could not even really enjoy waltzing with anyone but him. It was absolutely humiliating!

## CHAPTER 11

The next several days passed quickly. Emily did
not ask for the carriage. She dared not frequent
Bond Street for fear that Alexander might be lurk-
ing there. To meet the czar after what Dunstan
had said to her would be doing it up entirely too
brown. She occupied herself about the house, did
some needlework, read the latest French novel,
and waited for her new gown to arrive. She was
hoping that Dunstan would like her gown and
that Alexander would be gone from the city by
the time of the ball.

On the third morning after the trip to Almack's,
Emily entered Sarah's room to find her friend in
tears. "Sarah! What ever is the matter?"

Sarah wiped at her eyes. "It's—it's nothing. I'm just feeling weepy."

By now Emily had noticed the note in Sarah's hand. "Sarah Parker," she said sternly, "don't tell me any such Banbury tales. You're holding a note from Bersford and it looks like bad news."

Sarah made no further effort to hide her distress. "It is Bersford," she said. "His parents are still against the match, and we shall have to wait another year until he comes into some money left by his uncle. Oh, Emily, I am frightened. I don't want to lose him again."

"Now, Sarah." Emily was a little surprised to see how well she could function as a consoling friend. "Don't fret yourself. All sorts of things may happen to let you marry sooner. You won't lose Bersford, dear. He loves you."

Sarah seemed to perk up at this and Emily continued in the same vein until she had jollied her friend into better spirits. Then, when Sarah was once again her complacent self, Emily smiled. "I have some correspondence that I must attend to this morning. You will not go down in the dumps again, will you?"

Sarah returned her smile. "No, Emily. I am better. It's ungrateful of me to feel sad when I have so very much."

Emily nodded. "I'll see you later then."

As she made her way to her room, the plan that had been forming hazily in her mind began to take shape. She meant to write to Uncle Cyril to ask him to settle some of her inheritance on Sarah. *There must be a way to do it,* Emily thought, *a way so that Sarah would never know where the wonderful gift had come from.* Then she and Bersford could be happy. *After all,* thought Emily with a deep sigh, *someone should be happy.*

She settled at her writing desk and outlined her plan in a letter to Uncle Cyril. How very good it made her feel to be able to do something for her friend, she thought as she sealed the letter and rose to find a footman to send on its way. It was utterly stupid to let a thing like money separate two people who loved each other. There was enough difficulty around love, she thought as she sent Jeffers off to post the letter, without dragging money into the picture.

This done, she wandered restlessly from room to room, trying to dissipate the terrible longing for Dunstan that consumed her. And what, she told herself as she gazed out the window, would she do if Dunstan were here? She could not run into his arms where she felt safe. She could not declare her love for him, a love that was now the whole center of her life. In fact, if he should appear now, they would most likely end at cuffs. They almost always did.

How strange, thought Emily as she moved back toward a bookshelf in search of a book, that her partiality for him should have grown stronger and stronger as it had. Of course, it had had a good start, nursed as it had been through the long winter. It had certainly been quite strong that day when he passed her on the road, but now it was doubly strong and she knew no way to combat it. In fact, she had given up trying. No other man seemed at all appealing in the role of husband.

A slight sound at the door caused her to turn. Parks stood there, looking rather disconcerted. "Yes, Parks?"

"You've a caller, miss, a Lord Gilcrest."

"Gilcrest!" Emily's hand flew to her mouth. How had the man dared to come here!

She stared at Parks in bewilderment. "I don't understand. Has his lordship left any instructions in the matter?"

Parks frowned. "Lord Gilcrest has never been a caller here, miss. I've no idea what the viscount's wishes are."

Emily felt her heart pounding. She did not want to be rude, but she did not want to see Gilcrest. She most especially did not want to make Dunstan angry with her again. "Please, Parks?" She appealed to the old butler.

His face cleared. "Well, miss, if you don't wish to see the gentleman, you may be out." He frowned. "Though I should have known that sooner so as to tell him right off. Or you could have a headache and be indisposed."

"That's it, Parks." Emily beamed. "Oh, what a blessing you are. I have a headache, such a headache as no one has ever known. Do hurry and tell him so."

"Yes, miss. Right away." With a smile of obvious satisfaction, Parks departed to do his duty.

Emily sank into a chair, her legs trembling. She had no wish to see Gilcrest, especially if it meant that Dunstan would be angry. How could he be otherwise, she thought, considering the animosity that existed between the two men.

She spent some moments speculating on the nature of the tension that she had observed between the two, but was no nearer finding a reason for it when Parks reappeared. "Lord Gilcrest sent his regrets and wishes for your speedy recovery. He will call again tomorrow."

Emily caught her breath. How persistent the man was!

"Thank you, Parks. You've been a big help."

"You're quite welcome, miss," returned the butler and something about the expression on his face led Emily to wonder if Parks had knowledge of this matter between Dunstan and Gilcrest. But she dared not ask him. Parks returned to his duties and Emily was left to muse on the intricacies of life.

She was still musing when a deep voice sounded behind her. "So, you are at home."

Emily turned to see the viscount staring at her.

"Of course I am, I didn't request the carriage," she replied in surprise.

"No, you didn't." He came into the room and took a chair, but he did not stretch out in his usual lazy fashion. Instead he sat upright in the chair, as though he might leave it at any moment.

"Did you expect me to be gone?" asked Emily curiously. There was obviously something on Dunstan's mind.

He seemed to ignore her question. "I met Gilcrest's carriage on the street," he said, as though to no one in particular. "I wondered whom he was calling on."

So that was it, thought Emily. "Lord Gilcrest was here," she said calmly, waiting for his explosion. "He came to see me."

"Ah! And did you have a pleasant visit?" The decided edge to his tone took all the politeness from his request.

"Unfortunately, we did not," replied Emily, sure now that she had made the right decision. "I did not see Lord Gilcrest since I had Parks tell him that I was suffering from a headache."

"A marvelous expedient, a headache," he said, relaxing in his chair. "But even better is the simple statement that you are out."

"You are quite right," returned Emily crisply. "But unfortunately, I did not expect unwanted callers and therefore had left no word with Parks.

This being the case, he was constrained to announce my visitor."

"I see." For several long moments Dunstan remained silent, his eyes fixed on the fireplace painting.

In vain Emily waited for some further word of approbation. Couldn't he at least say well done?

"Lord Gilcrest informed Parks that he would return tomorrow," she added and waited.

His lordship did not resume his upright position. He remained perfectly still, and yet he no longer seemed relaxed. It was some moments, however, before he asked, "And how will you greet him?"

"I shall be out," said Emily firmly. "I shall be out whenever Lord Gilcrest calls."

Again the viscount did not move, yet she was aware that he was no longer tense. She waited until she could stand it no longer and then asked, "Does that decision meet with your approval, milord?"

Suddenly Dunstan got to his feet. "It does. And I hope you stick to it."

How like him, thought Emily angrily. Even when she did the right thing she was suspect.

She, too, stood and moved to face him. "It would be truly kind of you, if one day you should give me credit for a little common sense."

He stared at her in surprise, as though there

were no reason for her anger. "I do not under-stand."

"I should think that under the circumstances you might at least say well done. I was quite taken by surprise when Lord Gilcrest called, yet I had sense enough to come up with an excuse not to see him." She did not think it necessary to mention Parks's part in the matter. After all, the decision had been hers. "Knowing your antipathy for the man, I refused to see him. I respected your wishes in every way. I even refuse to see him in the future. Yet do you give me any praise, any indication that you are pleased with my behavior? No. Instead you still eye me with suspicion. It is insupportable!"

As she spoke, she worked herself into a state of agitation. Of course it was not merely the viscount's stupidity in this regard that infuriated her, but also his general refusal to see her as the woman she was. But she dared not voice that.

She stood before him indignantly, her breast rising and falling with the force of her emotion. He eyed her carefully for a moment and then he spoke soberly. "I beg your apology, Miss Penthorne. I have been lax in my behavior. I thank you for pointing it out to me. Certainly one who attempts to guide another into better paths should indicate his pleasure when that guidance is followed."

Somehow these were not the words Emily had

wished to hear, and she continued to glare at him until suddenly he chuckled and his dark eyes grew warm with laughter. "All right, Emily. Well done, very well done. There, does that please you?"

She nodded, though the truth was she still felt like hitting him. "That's better," she said stiffly. "But it would have been much nicer if I hadn't had to prompt you."

He continued to smile at her. "Come, Emily, relax. You are not following your own advice."

This surprised her into asking, "Why, what do you mean?"

He drew his features into a picture of woe. "I have done what you wanted and yet you continue to treat me as an ingrate."

Suddenly Emily burst into laughter. She was quite bewildered by it herself, for only moments ago she had been very angry with him. Yet there was truth in what he had said, a great deal of truth.

"There now," he said as she finished laughing. "I'm sure we both feel better. Not only that, we have reached a better understanding." He took her hand in his. "Have we not, Emily?"

He was so very close to her; her heart pounded in her throat and her fingers trembled in his. "Have we not?" he repeated, his dark eyes probing hers.

Emily managed a little smile. "Yes, milord, we have."

"Good. In the future we shall deal much better together. You shall see." With a squeeze he released her hand.

"Now, I must go. I have an appointment some distance away. Has your new gown arrived yet for Lady Cholmondoley's ball?"

Emily shook her head. "Not yet, milord. I expect it tomorrow."

He nodded. "That's fine. I look forward to seeing it on you that night." Then he was gone, out the door and down the hall before the import of his words struck. He looked forward to seeing it on her the night of the ball, he had said. That meant that he did not intend to pass judgment on it first.

She sat down suddenly, a curious weakness in her legs. That meant that he trusted her judgment in choosing the gown. What an important thing that seemed to her. It meant a great deal to be deemed worthy of his trust. Now she might have hope for the future. Some day he might recognize her for the woman she was. The thought sent her heart pounding.

But the serpent of suspicion stirred in her breast. He had seen the *modiste,* and told her what was acceptable. He had no reason for concern. He could afford this magnanimous gesture of respect. It cost him nothing.

All Emily's elation fled. And why was he dining out? she asked herself bitterly. Would he be with Harriette Wilson and her brilliant incognitas? Or was he somewhere else, in the apartments of that young woman in blue who had so captivated him at Almack's?

Emily rose from her chair and moved to the window. She was being ridiculous, she told herself sternly. Every time Dunstan left the house he need not be going to an assignation. Certainly he had other affairs to attend to. Yet he was such a fine figure of a man. At the theater and at Almack's it had not escaped her notice that more than one woman was taken by the viscount's dark good looks. He was a man and he knew Harriette Wilson. There remained little more to be said.

Emily's joy of a few moments previous turned to ashes as she sighed and went to seek out Parks. Regardless of her anger at Dunstan, she did not wish to see Lord Gilcrest. There was something very disquieting about the man, something more than Dunstan's dislike, that made her wish to avoid him altogether. She went to inform Parks that in the future she was always to be out to Lord Gilcrest.

## CHAPTER 12

Finally the evening of Lady Cholmondoley's ball arrived. Standing before her cheval glass, Emily was filled with excitement. Critically her eyes examined the self-ruching at the neck of her gown. Yes, all was well there. The gown fit perfectly. She ignored the other jewels in her chest and took out the pearls. Tonight she must do nothing to offend him. Tonight must be perfect.

She had her hair done in a new style—Roman it was called, with the tresses brought together and confined at the back of the head and ending in ringlets. She hoped the viscount would like it. With one last look, she turned away and picked up her cashmere threaded with blue. It would do no good to stand around wondering about his reactions. Far better to go down and discover them.

As she made her way down the stairs, his lordship came out of the library and stood watching her. She felt the color flood her cheeks, but she continued to descend steadily. He was wearing his corbeau-colored coat with covered buttons, his white marcella waistcoat, and black Florentine silk breeches. Her heart beat faster at the sight of him. Surely every woman at Lady Cholmondoley's would envy her. And for so little, she thought with a sigh. For no matter what she did, she could never get him to look at her as he had that first time—purely man to woman.

His eyes moved slowly over her and she fought to keep her composure. If there was something wrong with her gown—or her hair . . . She held her breath.

Then he smiled and gave her a slight bow. "Your dress is quite becoming. You chose well. And you have done your hair a new way."

"Yes, milord." Emily waited. He liked the gown, but what about her hair? Suddenly it seemed important to know. "Do you like it?" she stammered.

The viscount nodded. "It suits you admirably."

This compliment so took her breath away that she could not think of a reply. Fortunately Sarah appeared at that moment.

His lordship took Emily's cashmere from over her arm and placed it carefully around her shoulders. As he did so, his gloved fingers touched the nape of her neck and sent a shiver coursing down her spine.

She considered her reaction as the carriage moved through the streets of London. Why was it that when he touched her these strange feelings arose in her? Did every woman feel that at the touch of his fingers? There were no answers to these questions, of course, but they served to occupy Emily's mind until the slow pace of the carriage aroused her. Looking out, she saw that the crush of carriages before Lady Cholmondoley's mansion was terrible, but eventually the driver maneuvered them into place and the viscount helped the women from the carriage. The links blazing in their wrought-iron holders made the scene bright. Diamonds and other jewels sparkled as lords and ladies hurried up the walk.

"So many people," murmured Emily.

"The top of the *ton*," said his lordship with a lazy smile. "London's best. Lady Cholmondoley always insists on the best." He cast her a strange look as he said this, and Emily's heart skipped a beat. Could he be referring to the first time he had seen her in this very house?

Her heart pounded at the thought, but surely she must be mistaken. Most likely he did not remember that evening at all. She sighed. If only he did, perhaps things would be different.

They were greeted by Lady Cholmondoley,

whose diamonds, if possible, outshone those of her guests, and then they were left alone in the gathering throng.

Emily, on Dunstan's arm, tried to see if there was anyone present that she knew. She fully intended to refuse to dance with Lord Gilcrest, just as she had refused to receive him when he called. Hopefully he had not been invited. Nor the Emperor Alexander. She wished never to be bothered with either of them again.

The orchestra had already begun to play and the intoxicating rhythm of the waltz beat in Emily's blood. Perhaps Lord Byron was right about it inducing wantonness in young women. Certainly it was a great deal of fun. She turned to Dunstan, but almost as though he knew her thought and intended to forestall her, he disengaged his arm. "I see someone with whom I must speak. I shall return shortly."

He left her with Sarah. Emily attempted conversation with her companion, but Sarah was waiting for Bersford's arrival and her conversation reflected this fact.

Finally Emily turned her attention to the dancing. And then she saw it! Dunstan was waltzing—with that brazen creature from Almack's! This time her dress was of palest green and clung to her in a way that spoke most eloquently of damped petticoats.

Emily's heart sank. He had abandoned her in

162

order to dance with that terrible creature—and after she had done everything possible to please him. It just wasn't fair! Her body yearned for a waltz. Even more than that, she yearned to be close to him, to feel his heart beating under her ear and his arms around her. Now he was holding someone else.

She turned away in disgust. "Come, Sarah, let us look in the other room." Sarah followed, but her eyes kept straying toward the entrance.

The card room was more than half filled, mostly with dowagers intent on their games of piquet and loo. There was hardly a youngish woman in the room. They were all in the ballroom enjoying themselves, Emily thought enviously.

She sighed deeply and turned away again. She was even more conspicuous here than in the ballroom. She would dance with anyone who asked her, she thought somewhat angrily—even with Gilcrest.

At that moment she heard Sarah's muted cry of delight and knew that Bersford had arrived. For a few minutes Emily forgot her discomfort in considering how soon she could reasonably expect Uncle Cyril to respond to her letter. Shortly after that, Emily assumed, Sarah would be making wedding plans and she would have to look for a new companion.

She was startled out of her thoughts by the sound of a male voice and looked up to see a strange, elegantly dressed young man standing before her. It was a moment before recognition dawned. "Cousin Percy?"

The young man nodded. "And you are Emily." He shook his head. "What wonders three years' growth can do for a scrawny girl."

Emily grinned. She and Uncle Cyril's son, Percy, had been childhood companions, but in the last few years had not seen each other.

Percy took her hand. "Shall we have a waltz for old times' sake? You have made it to Almack's, I presume."

Emily nodded. "Yes, I may waltz without censure."

She felt her spirits rising. She and Percy had always had fun together. Some of it had been almost mischief, in fact.

"And so," said Percy, as he guided her expertly around the floor, "you have been making a name for yourself."

In her surprise Emily almost missed a step. "I?"

Percy chuckled. "You've got Dunstan for a guardian. Half London's young ladies and a goodly portion of the older ones are out to snare him. And you've got the Emperor Alexander hot on your heels. Really, Coz, that was an excellent idea. To drop your handkerchief right into his hand! And such excellent aim!"

"Percy, I didn't! It was an accident, really it was."

Percy laughed. "If it really was an accident, Coz, then I counsel you not to say so. Your reputation is already made."

Emily sighed. There was no use in telling Percy that she did not want such a reputation. It was clear that he had adopted the values of the worst part of the *ton* and would not understand her feelings on the matter, let alone those of the viscount.

The waltz was soon over and Percy returned her to Sarah's side. From the sort of looks that her companion gave him Emily could see that news of Percy's reputation had gone before him. Evidently Sarah knew more about him than Emily did. It was obviously not good.

"I will leave you to the rest of the bucks now," said Percy with a devilish grin that told her he was quite aware of Sarah's disapproval. "I must go in search of a little bird I am currently pursuing."

Sarah shook her head as he strode away and Emily found herself hoping that the little bird was not an innocent one. Percy's charm could disarm one to the point where it absolutely befuddled the line between right and wrong—as she had known more than once, and to her regret, when they were children.

She looked around for a sign of Dunstan, but before she could spot him in the crowd, another man was waiting to dance with her. Emily ac-

cepted him with a smile. There was little point
in wondering about Dunstan. Here she did not
have to compete with Harriette Wilson, since incognitas would not be invited to such a place.
But, of course, that brazen creature from Almack's probably still had him in tow. For the
hundredth time Emily wondered who that young
woman could be.

She did not see Dunstan during that dance nor
during the several sets of quadrilles that she
danced with other partners. But sometime toward
the middle of the evening as she was being whirled
around the floor, she saw him again. He was waltzing with a small, delicate woman with a tumble of
jet black curls and with dark brown eyes under
thick lashes. The Princess Lieven. Emily remembered having seen her at Almack's. A person was
apt to remember a patroness; they wielded a great
deal of power. Why did Dunstan dance with her?
What was she to him? Emily immediately began
to torment herself with such wonderings.

This kind of thinking was absolutely futile, she
told herself as the music stopped. It was ridiculous
to be so suspicious of Dunstan. At any rate, he had
a perfect right to have a woman. The thought gave
her cold shivers and she pushed it away.

As her partner began to lead her back to where
Sarah waited, there was a sudden hush in the
room. Looking up, Emily saw the reason for it.
Alexander the First, Emperor of Russia, had ar-

rived. He stood in the doorway, resplendent in his green velvet uniform, blazing with jeweled orders. He was quite an attractive man, thought Emily dispassionately. But to her he meant nothing, nothing at all.

She saw the Princess Lieven move to meet him and close behind her went Dunstan and that creature from Almack's. Anger blazed high in Emily's heart. He was very good at issuing orders to her, she thought bitterly, but he had no care for his own reputation. The woman beside him clung to his arm in a way that to Emily's shocked eyes seemed openly wanton. He did not even reprimand her.

Emily turned away. Let Alexander ask her to dance. Oh, she hoped he would. She would say yes. Let Dunstan think about that for a while!

She accepted invitations to dance from several more men and then she looked up to find Alexander standing before her. "You are quite lovely tonight, Miss Penthorne," he said, his heavily accented voice carrying to those who stood nearby. "The most beautiful woman in the room."

"You are most kind," said Emily, feeling the color flood her cheeks. If only Dunstan would say things like that to her. How pleased she would be.

"Will you join me in a waltz?" asked Alexander with a warm smile.

Emily hesitated. She knew Alexander was dangerous, but what could the man do on a crowded dance floor? And there was Dunstan, with that brazen creature hanging on him, daring to criticize her.

"Of course, your majesty. I should be honored." Emily put her hand in his and allowed him to lead her onto the floor.

As he gathered her into his arms, she felt an instinctive urge to draw back, but she conquered it. She must learn to appreciate the attentions of other men, for it seemed that she would not get those of Dunstan.

Alexander swept her expertly around the floor and Emily was aware that many eyes were upon them. She certainly hoped that the viscount was getting a good look.

"So," said Alexander. "We are the subject of much talk."

"We are?" replied Emily softly. "Why?"

Alexander laughed. "You are very good, Miss Penthorne. How well you play the innocent young miss."

"I am innocent," protested Emily.

Alexander laughed again. "The world thinks otherwise. The world is quite sure that we have already been, as they say, *tête-à-tête*."

"But we have not."

"Ah," said the emperor, "that is knowledge known only to us."

Emily had no reply to this. She had absolutely no intention of doing anything more than waltz with this man; she wished there was some way to convince him of it.

"We have already the reputation," continued Alexander smoothly. "It is a pity that we have not the pleasure of earning it."

"I believe you are mistaken in me, your majesty. I tried to tell you this before. My dropping the handkerchief was an accident, nothing more. How can I convince you of that?"

Alexander chuckled. "You Englishwomen. You like always the little games. Perhaps for you the truth is too blunt. Russian woman, French woman, ahhhhh! She admits to the pleasures of the flesh. Admits and delights."

"That may well be," returned Emily stiffly. "But I am neither French nor Russian, and I am not playing games with you. I mean exactly what I say."

Alexander ignored this and swept her into a series of dips and turns that left her breathless. "I look for you at Bond Street," he said genially. "But you do not come."

"And I won't." She put this as strongly as she could, but again he refused to respond. Did he never hear anything that went against what he wished? Emily wondered.

For some moments he was silent, concentrating

on the waltz. Then he again led her through intricate and involved steps that left her panting for breath and slightly dizzy.

After one of these particularly intricate circles, he suddenly waltzed her through an open French door and out into the garden.

Emily's head was spinning from the dance and she did not realize what had happened until the texture of the floor changed beneath her feet to that of grass. "Your majesty!" she began, but Alexander had already pulled her behind a convenient tree and into his arms.

Emily considered screaming, but it would be quite ridiculous to bring Lady Cholmondoley's guests into the scene, and Dunstan would be furious. No, she must get out of this herself.

"Please, let me go! I should not be here."

Alexander chuckled. "Ah, little one. Your protests do not fool me. I have read your desire in your eyes."

Emily swallowed a half-hysterical giggle. What fools men could be! Alexander was obviously so enamored of himself that he could not conceive of a woman who might really refuse him.

She wondered if she should struggle, but at the moment that would only make him hold her tighter. Perhaps if she bided her time, even appeared to acquiesce, he might loosen his grip and she could slip away from him.

"Please, your majesty, do not hold me quite so closely. I find I feel rather faint."

Alexander was all solicitude. "My little one. The excitement, it is too much for you. Gently, we will go gently."

Emily, murmuring something indistinguishable, was struck again by the man's colossal conceit. He obviously believed that he had a tremendous effect on her. Well, she thought grimly, let him continue to think so until she had a chance to get away.

The strains of the music floated out to them and the night air was warm. If only, thought Emily, if only it were Dunstan whose arms encircled her so closely.

Then Alexander moved one of his arms and his hand sought her chin. "We will have a little kiss now," he whispered. "A foretaste of the pleasures to come."

As his lips came closer to hers, she shifted her balance in order to stamp on his foot. Then from behind Alexander's head a deep voice said calmly. "Ah, Emily. Here you are. Come, my dear, it is time to leave."

Alexander's arms fell away from her and for a moment Emily was stunned. How had Dunstan found them there? But there was no time for speculation. Dunstan stood waiting. His face was calm but a patch of light from the ballroom revealed the telltale twitching of the muscle in his jaw.

"Of course, milord. I am ready." She tried to make her tone as even as his own, for it had suddenly occurred to her that the viscount's position was very difficult. He could not call out the Emperor of Russia, but he was responsible for the honor of his ward.

She cursed the foolishness that had made her consent to that dance with Alexander. "You have met the emperor, Dunstan?" she asked, carrying on the charade of polite innocence.

"Yes," he replied. "Good evening, your majesty."

He offered her his arm and led Emily back into the ballroom. Not a word was spoken as he led her across the floor to where Sarah and Bersford sat fondly chatting. "Emily has a headache," he announced in a tone that utterly defied contradiction. "We must leave immediately." He turned to Bersford. "Perhaps you would care to accompany us."

"I would indeed," replied that gentleman with a look at Sarah.

Emily saw from Sarah's look that her companion was aware that something was wrong, but there was no opportunity to talk privately.

The ride home seemed pleasant enough on the surface. Bersford, Sarah, and the viscount discussed the events of the evening—all except the important one of Emily's being found in the garden with Alexander—and Emily made a comment here and there. But she was not deceived by this simulated pleasantness. Dunstan was extremely angry and she was well aware of it. She was reprieved only until they reached the house on St. James's Square. Then the fur would fly. Of this she was quite certain.

They left Bersford in the carriage, which would carry him to his own rooms and at the foot of the stairs Dunstan bade Sarah good night. "Emily and I have a matter to discuss," he said. "She will be up later."

"Yes, milord." Sarah's creased forehead indicated her worry, but there was little Emily could do to reassure her. In fact, she was feeling rather fearful herself. In the full force of his wrath Dunstan was quite overpowering.

Emily followed the viscount obediently into the library and stopped. She felt somehow that she had better keep to her feet. He was not quite so intimidating that way.

He shut the door with a thud and turned to face her. For long moments his eyes raked her over. Emily's heart rose up in her throat as she tried to persuade herself that she was not frightened.

"So," he said finally. "So, you disregard all my pleas to your common sense and go sneaking about in the garden with Alexander."

"I was not sneaking." She was dismayed to find that her voice wanted to crack. "I didn't even know we were going there until we were already there."

Plainly he did not believe her. His dark brows drew together into a terrible frown. "Do not play the innocent with me!" he thundered. "I warned you about Alexander. You had more than ample warning as to the nature of the man. Yet you waltzed with him and allowed yourself to be alone with him."

Emily struggled with her anger. Why must he always believe the worst where she was concerned? "I did not allow myself to be alone with him. He waltzed me into the garden unawares." She swallowed hastily and wished she had seated herself. Her knees were trembling violently, but she would not back down from him now.

Dunstan sighed. "I knew this was going to be a difficult job, but I never expected it to be this bad. You must be the wildest and most unpredictable girl in all London. Such wanton behavior makes my task of finding you a husband particularly arduous."

Emily drew herself up. Her anger at his unfairness was giving her new strength. "I am not a girl and I am not wild. As far as wanton goes"—her voice rose shrilly—"what about that brazen creature that was hanging on your arm?"

Dunstan's face darkened. "That is a matter altogether outside your concern. We will not discuss it."

Tears of rage rose to Emily's eyes. "This is grossly unfair. You are at liberty to badger and harass me all you please about the littlest and most inconsequential things. But I am to say nothing at all to you."

Dunstan glared at her. "You misstate the case. First, my behavior with Miss Castlemain or any other woman is no concern of yours. I am the guardian, not the other way around. Second, a man may do many things with impunity that a woman may not. For example, after tonight's escapade, Alexander will be as eagerly sought after as ever. His reputation will not have suffered at all. While yours—" His frown deepened further. "Very few people will be left who do not believe that Alexander has had his way with you."

"How absolutely ludicrous!" cried Emily. "Has the *ton* nothing better to do than to speculate on the private lives of others?"

"Probably not," he answered. "The fact remains that you have compromised your good name and I must still find you a husband. It will now be even more difficult than ever to find you a decent one."

"Perhaps I don't want a husband," cried Emily. "Men are all stupid. They don't believe the truth when it is told them. They always insist on having everything their own way. And they are terribly, terribly unfair!"

"You *must* have a husband," replied the viscount sternly. "You must have someone to take care of you, to protect you from men like Alexander."

Emily sniffed. "I would have handled Alexander. I would have gotten away from him by myself."

Dunstan's frown deepened. "Now you are being ridiculous. You could not have escaped the emperor's grasp."

"Oh? See? You are always so sure of yourself. I could have gotten away—quite easily in fact. And then that stupid man might have been finally convinced that I am not what he believes me to be." She glared at Dunstan.

"So, you can take care of yourself?" He eyed her speculatively.

Emily nodded. "Of course I can."

"Come here," he said suddenly.

Emily looked at him in puzzlement.

"Come here," he repeated.

There was something strange about his tone, something compelling. She hesitated and then moved toward him.

"So you can take care of yourself," he repeated.

"Yes, I can." Emily was uncomfortable being so close to him and moved to back away, but he reached out quickly and grabbed her arms.

"Suppose we are at another ball where Alexander is. We most probably shall be, since we cannot turn down all social invitations while the man is in town. Suppose he tries to kiss you as he did tonight."

"Suppose he does," repeated Emily. "I shall stop him."

"Indeed!" Dunstan's eyes sparkled dangerously. Before she quite knew what was happening, he had swept her into his arms. "And how would you release yourself from this?" he asked, with the lazy smile of the rake.

Emily began to struggle, but soon found it useless. "I should scream," she replied, conscious that his closeness had caused the usual shortening of her breath and that she wanted to burrow into his chest.

"Oh, that would be fine. What a merry scandal that would cause and the emperor insulted on top of it. Now tell me, Miss Penthorne, what should you do if I offered to kiss you?"

Emily, her heart pounding in her throat, could not reply. She did attempt to keep him from reaching her lips, but he clasped her to him with one hand and used the other to turn her chin toward him. The thought moved fleetingly through her mind that she should stamp on his foot as she had intended to stamp on Alexander's, but then his lips covered hers.

It was the first kiss Emily had ever known, and

it sent her senses trembling off into ecstasy. The kiss was brutal and savage; evidently Dunstan meant it as a learning experience for her. But she did not care. It was only with the greatest difficulty that she kept herself from returning it wholeheartedly. As it was, as his mouth continued to linger on hers, as the kiss turned more tender and persuasive, she felt her legs begin to go weak and her mouth soften under his.

Then, quite abruptly, he put her from him. If possible, his frown was even more ferocious. "You do not seem to have been very effective in freeing yourself from my attentions," he said dryly. "May I suggest that most men would be at least equally experienced? I believe that I will suspend your privileges to the carriage for a few days. I do not want you about on the streets while Alexander is still in the city."

Emily, her heart still pounding in her throat, felt anger rising in her. How terribly unfair he was. "I did not invite the attentions of the emperor," she cried angrily. "Nor would I ever be senseless enough to have a rendezvous with him or any other man. And, as to your lesson in kissing, perhaps you are right. I am not very effective at escaping a kiss that is forced upon me. But then, a kiss is a very little thing after all, is it not?"

She was herself appalled as the words left her mouth and she did not even know why she had said them, unless it was some urge to hit back at him. Certainly they had angered him even further. For a moment it looked as though he meant to commit violence on her person.

"A kiss may seem a very little thing to you," he said angrily, "but I assure you that to most men it is not. If you allow a man to kiss you, he will soon expect other liberties—unlawful ones."

Emily felt her cheeks flame. "You are being unfair again," she cried. "Alexander did not kiss me. No man has kissed me but you!" The pulses pounded in her throat as she stared at him. "Am I now to expect further unlawful liberties from you?" she taunted him. "Or has this lesson in manners ended?"

Dunstan took a step toward her and she feared that he would shake her as he had that time before, but she staunchly held her ground. "The lesson is ended," he said curtly. "I can only hope you have the good sense to profit from it!" Still glaring, he marched from the room.

Emily sank into a nearby chair, her legs no longer capable of holding her, and dropped her head into her hands. Things between them were growing worse and worse. He had all but accused her of being wanton! And yet she had done nothing—nothing at all to earn that appellation. The tears came then; there was no keeping them back. Her case seemed more and more hopeless with every passing day. Though her love for him grew stronger and stronger, she seemed never able to convince him to see her as a woman grown and worthy of his regard. Then, her lips still bruised from his kiss, she rose and hurried up the stairs to the privacy of her room. It was time for a good cry and there was no point in doing it in public.

## CHAPTER 13

In the days that followed Emily grew no more hopeful. Several men came to call. She received them, endured their visits with as much grace as possible, and told Dunstan that they were unsuitable as husbands. Surprisingly he did not seem to take this badly. Once, in fact, she thought she caught a look of relief on his face.

Emily did her best to cause no more trouble with the viscount. When Gilcrest came repeatedly to call, he was just as repeatedly informed that Miss Penthorne was out. And when after Alexander left the city Dunstan said politely, "You may request the carriage at your convenience," she replied just as politely, "Thank you." But she did not often avail herself of that privilege. She had an abundance of new clothes and there seemed little to shop for. She could not even get caught up in the general enthusiasm over the coming Victory Celebration decreed by the Prince Regent to take place on August first.

She was also experiencing a new sense of loneliness. Viscount Bersford came often to call on Sarah, and Emily gave her companion more and more time to be alone with her beloved. She herself did not like to spend too much time with them. She thought perhaps it was because, in spite of the difficulties in the way of their match, they seemed sublimely happy. Though certainly Emily wished Sarah every happiness possible, it could not be denied that the sight of their joy made her own misery still more acute.

Emily spent a great deal of time by herself, wandering from room to room in the house, wondering how her life would turn out. She knew she would soon have to look for a new companion, a task she did not relish at all. But she could not begin the search until Sarah got the good news of her so-called inheritance.

Finally the day Emily had waited for with anticipation—and dread—arrived. A letter came for Sarah, a franked letter, but written in a strange hand. "Look, Emily," said her friend. "I wonder what that could be.

Emily looked at it carefully. "I don't know, Sarah. Why don't you open it and see?"

Sarah nodded. "Of course. It just seems strange. I mean, I have no one to write to me. This is not Bersford's hand."

She tore open the letter and began to read. Halfway through she suddenly sat down and murmured, "Dear God!"

Emily's pretended innocence of the letter's contents vanished and she began to feel real concern. Perhaps this wasn't the letter she had expected.

Sarah finished reading and sat as one dazed. Finally Emily could wait no longer. "Sarah, whatever is it? You look so pale."

"It's—it's a letter from a solicitor—a Mr. Patterson. He says . . ." She shook her head as though still not believing it. "He says that I have been left an inheritance—a thousand pounds."

"Oh, Sarah!" Emily's relief was genuine. "You had me so frightened. I thought something terrible had happened."

"No, no. It's just—I can't believe it."

Emily ran to her friend. "Oh, Sarah, do you know what this means?"

Sarah stared at her from dazed eyes. "What, Emily? I still cannot believe it. A cousin I never heard of. It seems unreal."

"Oh, Sarah!" Emily pulled her friend to her feet and gave her a hug. "Think! Think what it means! It means that you and Bersford needn't wait. You can call the banns immediately."

Sarah's face broke into a slow smile. Then she clapped her hands. "Of course! Oh, Emily, I didn't even think of that. I must send for Bersford." She clasped her friend to her. "Oh, Emily, this is wonderful news." There was a long pause. "But," said Sarah in the softest voice, "Bersford and I cannot marry. I cannot leave you."

Emily forced herself to smile. "Nonsense, Sarah. You will marry as soon as Bersford gets the banns called. I shall miss you, of course." She swallowed over the sudden lump in her throat. "But I am so pleased that you will be happy."

Sarah gave her another hug. "You are a sweet girl, Emily. I hope that soon you will find someone to love."

"I hope so, too," replied Emily. "But do hurry. You write the note and I shall call for Jeffers to deliver it. Listen, don't tell him all of it, just that it's good news. Then you can tell him the rest when he arrives and we will get to see his face."

"An excellent idea, Emily. Oh, I can hardly wait!"

The note was soon dispatched and Emily and Sarah sat down to wait. But they could not sit still. They jumped up and ran to the window at the slightest sound, and then were reduced to giggles at their actions.

It was thus that Dunstan came upon them, their heads close together as they peered through the

curtained window. "So," he said, "are you ex-
pecting someone special?"

Emily thought that his eyes were turned on
her. "We're waiting for Bersford," she said. "The
most marvelous thing has happened. Sarah has
just received news of an inheritance. It means
that she and Bersford may marry."

Dunstan's face lit up. "What excellent news!
Miss Sarah, may I offer my congratulations?"

"Yes, thank you, milord. I—I am quite beside
myself with joy."

"You deserve to be happy," said Dunstan.

"We are waiting to tell Bersford." Emily could
not help bubbling a little with happiness for her
friend. "She wrote him only that she had good
news."

"Good news of what?" came Bersford's voice
from the doorway. "You're sure nothing is wrong?
I came posthaste."

Sarah hurried to his side. "Bersford, oh, do look!
Emily, Emily, where is the letter?" She looked
around her, entirely unlike the usual calm and
collected Sarah.

"Here it is, Sarah, right where we left it." Emily
passed the letter on to her friend.

"See, Bersford, an inheritance. It means—" Sarah
flushed, unable to go on.

"It means we can call the banns!" Bersford so
far forget himself as to take Sarah into his arms,
but when she protested, he released her.

"Do not be embarrassed," said his lordship. "After all, your alliance will soon be a matter of common knowledge."

Sarah flushed. "You are so kind, milord."

The viscount smiled. "Come, Emily, I believe we have a matter to discuss in the library."

For a moment Emily looked at him in surprise, but, when he slowly lowered an eyelid, she hurried to agree. "Of course, milord. Right away."

She followed him out of the room, leaving Sarah and her Bersford some privacy in which to celebrate their happiness.

"We do have a matter to discuss," said the viscount as he took a chair and Emily settled on a sofa. "We must find you a new companion."

Emily nodded. "It will be very difficult to replace Sarah. I doubt that it can be done."

His lordship smiled gravely. "She has certainly been a good friend to you."

Emily nodded. Now that her first feelings of elation for her cousin were passing, she could feel that sense of impending emptiness. Life would be doubly hard without Sarah's companionship. Waves of desolation swept over her in a rush, leaving her choked with tears. She stifled a sob.

She tried to turn her head so that he would not hear, but Dunstan was too quick for her. He was at her side in an instant. "Emily, my dear girl. What is it?"

Emily fought valiantly, but she could not keep

back the tears. "I—I'm sorry. I know it's—silly," she sobbed. "But I shall miss Sarah so. No one can ever replace her." In spite of all her efforts to restrain them, the tears continued to stream down her cheeks.

Dunstan took a clean cambric square from his pocket and offered it to her. "It's natural for you to feel sorrow in this situation. But soon you will have a husband of your own."

This caused Emily to break into fresh tears. She could never marry another while she loved Dunstan. "I—I don't think so," she sobbed. "I—I feel so alone, so terribly alone."

The viscount put his arm around her. "You are not alone, Emily. I am here and I care about you. Do not forget that."

He cared about her, she thought, but not in the way she wanted him to. Right now, for instance, she wanted desperately for his arm to tighten around her possessively, but of course it would not. The thought made her break into fresh tears.

He gathered her against his striped waistcoat. "Go ahead and cry, Emily. Life is not always easy, even for those of us who are well placed."

For long moments Emily sobbed in his arms, crying not just for the loss of Sarah, but for the love that she felt would never be consummated. If only there were some way, any way, that she could get him to love her. But that seemed impossible.

Dunstan let her cry for some time in peace. Then he spoke. "Come, Emily. Sarah will not be gone completely. She and Bersford will have a place in London. You will see her often."

Emily nodded. "I know, but it will not be the same."

"Life changes," said Dunstan soberly. "There is no way we can stop it. We can only accept the change and go on."

Emily nodded. She could not tell him that most of her sorrow was due to her love for him, love that seemed fated never to be returned.

"Now, Emily, dry your eyes. Next week we shall go to the Victory Celebration. I have tickets for us for St. James's Park. You shall see the Chinese pagoda and the fleet of miniature warships. There will be fireworks and balloonists, all sorts of amusing things to see."

Obediently Emily wiped her eyes. "Shall we go to the celebration together?" she asked.

"Of course. And your Sarah and Bersford shall accompany us. We shall make a gala evening of it."

Emily nodded, her spirits rising a little. It would be fun to have an outing together now that Alexander had gone back to Russia—presumably to pursue Russian women, she thought with a slight smile.

"There, that's much better. There's really a great deal to be cheerful about." He regarded her solemnly. "Especially since you were able to achieve your purpose without Sarah suspecting anything."

Emily stared at him in surprise. "What do you mean?"

Dunstan smiled warmly. "Since I am your guardian here, Uncle Cyril advised me of your plan to help Sarah. I find it very thoughtful of you."

Emily felt herself reddening. "I did not mean for anyone to know," she murmured.

"I don't see why not," replied Dunstan. "It can only redound to your credit."

"But Sarah must not know," Emily cried. "She must never know. She is so proud. Please," she pleaded, "say you won't tell her—or Bersford either."

"All right, Emily, I will not give you away."

"Thank you, milord." Emily heaved a sigh of relief. "You see, I know Sarah and she would refuse the money. I'm sure she would, if she knew it was from me. I know she wants the best for me."

Dunstan smiled strangely. "And what about you, Emily? Aren't you afraid that the loss of a thousand pounds will lower your chances in the marriage mart?"

Emily sniffed. "I don't really care. If a man only wants me for my money, I'd as soon not have him." She sighed again. "I just wish I could find someone as good as Sarah to be my friend. But I don't see how I can."

Dunstan patted her hand. "I suppose we should put out an advertisement, unless you have someone in mind. A needy relative?"

Emily shook her head. "I know of no one else in the family." She paused. "Cousin Percy may know of someone."

"Uncle Cyril's son?" It was plain from his tone that Dunstan did not regard Percy as the dearest of friends.

Emily nodded. "We played together as children. He was at Lady Cholmondoley's the other night."

"Ah, yes. An elegantly dressed young buck."

"Yes, Cousin Percy is quite the charmer." Emily smiled.

"I trust he has not charmed you." There was something in his voice that caused her to raise her head in surprise.

She laughed. "Indeed, not. I am onto all of Percy's wiles. However, in the old days he often used to lead me into mischief." She shook her head. "Things always seemed so simple the way Percy explained them. Until we got caught."

The viscount's body seemed to stiffen slightly. "Have you considered the young man as an alliance?"

"Percy?" Emily's voice rose merrily. "Percy as a husband?" She burst into laughter. "Dear God, I should not have a moment's peace in such a match. Why, I doubt not but what he'd lead the very children into mischief after him, he has such a knack for it." She shook her head. "No, Percy and I were childhood friends and playmates. That is the most we shall ever be to each other."

"I think that a wise decision," said Dunstan. "I know little of him firsthand, since I was at the front with Wellington when Percy went on the town. But what I hear secondhand does not at all convince me that he is good husband material."

Emily smiled. "If I know Percy, marriage is quite far from his thoughts. He is probably thinking only of enjoyment. He told me he was pursuing a little bird."

Dunstan did not smile. "That is the primary occupation of many young bucks these days, to the detriment of many innocent young women. I wish to find you a sober, sensible husband, one who will treat you decently."

"I thank you, milord, but I have seen no such man in all of London. The older men are all confirmed rakes, intimates of Harriette Wilson and her kind." She watched him closely but his expression did not change. "And the younger ones are all callow striplings, hardly worthy of the name man."

Dunstan looked at her strangely. "You seem rather cynical for such a young woman."

Emily sighed. "Perhaps I shall never marry.

Then you will be forced to act as my guardian forever."

The viscount chuckled. "Nonsense, Emily. The right man will come along. You will see."

To this Emily made no reply. She could scarcely tell him that the right man had come along—and that he was that man. No, she must simply go on and hope that some day, some way, he would learn to love her as she desired, with all the passion of a man for a woman.

She managed to smile at him. "I must admit, milord, that sometimes I despair. With men like Gilcrest—and Alexander—in the world, and even Percy, how can a woman be at all safe?"

"By having a husband," declared the viscount promptly. "Someone who will take good care of her."

"That is all well and good," replied Emily. "But where are such men to be found?"

Dunstan frowned slightly. "There are a few to he found still. Your Sarah found one in Bersford, did she not?"

Emily nodded. "Yes, that is true." She wiped at her face with Dunstan's handkerchief.

"Then," said the viscount, "you must not despair. Some good, decent man will come along, someone who genuinely cares about you. You will see."

Emily sighed and tried to look as though she believed him.

He got to his feet and pulled her up after him.

"Come, you must be merrier or you will spoil your Sarah's happiness."

Emily nodded. "I know. If she sees that I've been crying, I'll tell her it's for joy."

Dunstan squeezed her hand. "That's the girl, Emily." He glanced quickly at the mantel clock. "Now I must leave you. You will be all right, won't you? I simply cannot break this appointment and I am late already."

"Of course," lied Emily over the newly rising tears. "I shall be fine." She watched him go with head held high.

It was not until he was out of sight down the hall and she was about to break into tears again that the realization came. He was late for his appointment because he had stayed to comfort her. She was that important to him, she thought with a triumphant smile, important enough to make him late. Certainly that was a good beginning. Even if he was now on his way to see Harriette Wilson or that Castlemain girl, at least he was beginning to think of her. She made her way upstairs to wash her face. It was foolish to cry anymore, especially now that she had a faint glimmer of hope.

## CHAPTER 14

The morning of August first began with showers. Watching the drops coursing down the window-pane, Emily grew sadder with each rainy moment. How could they go to the park in such inclement weather? Everyone would be soaked through.

But gradually by noon the rain stopped and the sun came out. By the time they were ready to leave for St. James's Park and the regent's great Victory Celebration, the city had dried up considerably and was comfortably cool.

Emily was abubble with enthusiasm. She knew, however, that its origin was not the victory of the Allied Sovereigns over that rascally Napoleon. The cause for her joy was much closer to home. It seemed to her that since the day of Sarah's wonderful news, the day Dunstan had held her in his arms and comforted her, he looked at her differently. She could not say exactly how, but there was something different in their dealings with each other. From this simple fact she took a great deal of hope. Sarah and Bersford, the first calling of their banns done the previous Sunday, were free to exchange as many looks of love and devotion as they wished.

As the carriage proceeded through the London streets, getting closer to St. James's Park and the site of the celebration, Emily stared out the window in astonishment. Never had she seen the streets so packed with people. She turned startled eyes to Dunstan. "Look at the crowd. So many people."

Dunstan nodded. "All of London appears to be going to the Victory Celebration. All the shops are shut, everyone excused from working. I'm glad I have tickets for the seats in the enclosure; I should not like to have you jostled about by the common humanity."

Emily shivered. "Like those poor women at the king's big banquet. They lost their shoes, and some even their clothes, in the crush. How dreadful it must have been."

Dunstan agreed. "Mobs can be rather vicious, I'm afraid. There is something about the anonymity of a great mob that makes a man—or a woman—lose sight of common decency."

Emily found herself drawing closer to his lordship and flushed at the discovery.

He seemed to divine her reason and smiled comfortingly. "There is no need to be frightened, Emily." His hand reached over to cover hers momentarily and even through both their gloves she felt the warmth of his fingers. The blood rushed to her face again.

"I am not frightened. Not very much," she added truthfully. "It's just that with so many people, if a person should fall—why the crowd needn't even be angry. One could be trampled before anyone noticed." She shivered again as she saw mothers carrying infants and fathers with toddlers on their shoulders in the throngs that flooded the street.

"You just keep a hold on my arm," said Dunstan grimly, "and I guarantee you will not be trampled. That's a certainty."

"Thank you," said Emily. "I could never really be frightened when I'm with you."

Something strange appeared in his eyes for the briefest moment and then was gone. What had she seen there? Emily asked herself. Could it have been tenderness? But now his eyes had veiled over and they showed nothing.

Sarah spoke then and the moment was lost.

"From what the *Chronicle* said, the celebration should be something special."

Bersford nodded. "I myself am looking forward to seeing Sadler, the balloonist. That fellow has nerve." Bersford's plain face lit up with excitement.

Sarah turned to him in anxiety. "You are not thinking of doing such a thing, I hope, milord."

"No, no, of course not, my dear. I would not think of it, especially if it gave you any cause for alarm."

"It would, it certainly would." Sarah's expression made that quite clear.

"What about you?" Dunstan asked suddenly of Emily.

"What about me?" she asked in surprise.

His eyes sparkled at her. "Should you be frightened if I were to become a balloonist?"

Emily stared at him for a moment. Didn't he realize what that question sounded like? That it made it seem that they were—about to make an alliance? Her heart pounded in her throat.

"Well, milord," she said as calmly as she could. "If you should ever decide to become a balloonist, I should not dare to gainsay you." She smiled at him innocently. "After all, I am not your guardian." Some of the warmth in his eyes seemed to fade and she hurried on. "But if my relationship to you were that of Sarah to Bersford—" That something flickered in his eyes again. She was sure she saw it. "I should still not gainsay you. For I know that a balloon would not dare go against your will and you should be perfectly safe wherever you were."

"Emily," said Sarah with a soft smile. "It's clear that you are not in love."

Emily shook her head. "You are operating on a false premise, Sarah. A woman may love a man so much that she will not deny him anything that is important to him."

Sarah considered this for some moments and Emily felt herself coloring. Then Sarah shook her head. "I am sorry, Emily, but I could not do that."

Emily risked a glance at his lordship and found that he was surveying her closely. "That is quite a mature concept of love," he said softly as Sarah and Bersford returned to their own conversation. "I think that you have grown considerably in the last weeks."

Emily managed a small smile. "Perhaps I have always believed that about love," she said. "You have never asked me my opinion on the subject."

He continued to smile at her warmly. "You're quite right, Emily. It appears there are many things I don't know about you."

Emily caught her breath. "Our relationship has been somewhat—unusual," she said. "Not as ordinary man to woman."

The viscount nodded. "You are right. And we did not get off to the most admirable beginnings."

Emily, her heart pounding, replied softly, "No, we did not."

"But," he continued, "there is no need for us to remain at cuffs over everything."

"No," she replied, "there is no need."

His eyes met hers and held them and Emily felt her own eyes filling with tears. Just as it seemed that he was going to say something, the carriage drew to a halt. His eyes veiled over once again and he said politely, "Well, here we are at St. James's Park. You ladies had best bring your cloaks along. You may not need them now, but as the sun goes down the air may grow more chill."

Emily nodded. Dunstan was now so perfectly matter of fact. Could he have looked at her in that tender way only seconds before? She could not be sure. Maybe she was imagining the whole thing because she wanted to believe it.

Then they were climbing carefully out of the carriage. As she reached the ground, Emily stayed quite close to Dunstan. She noticed that he immediately took her arm and tucked it through his. She clung to him gratefully.

Sarah and Bersford were soon beside them and they moved off toward the gate. It was very slow going, for the area before the gate was packed with people of all kinds. Lords and ladies rubbed elbows with shop girls and chimney sweeps, tinkers and butchers' boys. Dunstan moved steadily through the throng, his broad shoulders and fierce countenance clearing a way for them. Beside him, his arm close to her, Emily felt surprisingly safe.

The Horse Guards at the gate nodded at seeing the tickets and Emily breathed a sigh of relief as they passed through and into the park. The crowd there was not so dense and it was somewhat easier to move about.

Dunstan paused and looked around them. "It seems wisest to go directly to the benches provided. As the crowd grows thicker it may be difficult to find a place to sit."

Bersford nodded. "That sounds like a good idea. I don't want Sarah to be jostled about."

"I expect you have taken precautions concerning your watch and other valuables," said Dunstan. "No doubt there are a great many divers on the lay here. Those who make their living picking pockets could ask for nothing better than a crowd like this."

Bersford nodded. "I took precautions before I left my room."

"Good." Dunstan moved off toward where the seats were arranged and Bersford and Sarah followed closely behind.

As the men settled them onto the benches, Emily looked around her. Though it was not as crowded as the streets, the park was full of people. Booths and open marquees had sprung up all over. The smell of frying meat hung in the air. There would be lots of good business on a day like this.

Emily smiled at the sight of two small boys shinnying up a tree to get a better view. Then she frowned. Where was the mother of those boys? How could she allow such small youngsters to run around by themselves? She turned to Sarah. "Look at those little boys."

Sarah nodded and Bersford smiled. "Little devils will get a good view up there."

"They seem very small to be out by themselves," said Emily.

Bersford looked at her in surprise. "Those little urchins? They've probably been on their own for years."

Emily remained quiet. The facts of London life had never been more clearly apparent. Her children, she thought silently, would never risk life and limb like that. She recalled her earlier words to Sarah and paused in her thinking. Perhaps if she really loved them, she would want to give her sons the freedom to do such things. Otherwise how could they learn and grow?

Dunstan touched her hand lightly. "Emily, you are looking extremely serious. What grave matters are presently occupying your mind?"

Emily flushed. "I was thinking of—the day when I have sons."

His dark eyes met hers. "Serious thoughts for a young woman not yet betrothed."

She nodded. Somehow it was very important for her to make him understand. "I was looking at those boys." She indicated the two urchins, who by now had moved far out on a limb and were bouncing there happily.

He nodded. "Yes, go on."

"First I thought I should not allow my sons to behave so dangerously. But then I remembered what I had said—about loving someone. And I realized that if I loved them, I should not want to protect them too much. I should want to give them room to grow and learn, even to make mistakes. Because that is a way of learning." She looked at him anxiously. "Does that make any sense to you?"

He looked at her thoughtfully. "Yes, it does. A great deal of sense." His gloved hand closed over hers again for the merest fraction of a second. "I am discovering more and more about you today," he said, that strange look flickering in his eyes again.

Emily caught her breath. There was something special between them. Surely she could not be imagining it.

Then Sarah tugged at her sleeve. "Look, Emily, look at the Chinese pagoda."

Emily really had no other choice but to look,

yet she was extremely loath to take her eyes away from Dunstan's. When he looked at her like that . . .

The pagoda appeared to have seven stories and was erected on a bridge over the canal. Why the peace should be celebrated with a pagoda was unclear to her, but then the Prince Regent's penchant for things Oriental was well-known. Everyone knew about the Chinese decorations of resplendent Brighton Pavilion, including its great Oriental dome. Emily lost herself in musing over what it was like to live in such magnificence.

Her inheritance made her sought after by many suitors, and she could well afford the thousand pounds that Uncle Cyril had helped her settle on Sarah. But she had never known the kind of splendor with which the prince surrounded himself. She thought it would probably be an inconvenience. She liked comfort, but too much opulence could be cloying.

Suddenly she was brought out of her musing by the stiffening of the man beside her. She looked up to find Lord Gilcrest standing before them. "Good afternoon, Miss Penthorne. I see that you are, as usual, out." Gilcrest's sharp face held only a suave smile. "I have left my card several times," he continued smoothly, "but it is my misfortune always to find you out."

Emily did not know how to reply to this and glanced instinctively at Dunstan. His face was calm, but she saw the telltale muscle twitching in his jaw.

"Some men might surmise, after such repeated misfortunes, that their calls were not wanted by the lady in question," Dunstan observed calmly.

Emily's heart jumped up into her throat. Surely Dunstan would not call this man out. But if Gilcrest should take offense . . .

"Indeed, Dunstan," Gilcrest replied cheerfully, "some men might. But I know better." His eyes met Emily's and he smiled. "Some day perhaps I shall be fortunate enough to have the lady listen to her heart instead of her keeper." With that comment he bowed low and coolly departed before Emily could think of a suitable reply.

She was aware of Dunstan's eyes on her and felt the color creep into her cheeks. "I—I will not receive him," she stammered. "He is . . ." She searched for the right words. "Not a good man. Something about him frightens me."

She could almost feel the tension leaving Dunstan's body at her words. Again she wondered at the source of the antagonism between the two men. She knew it had existed before her advent on the scene. Gilcrest's attentions to her had only served to increase an anger that had already existed.

A glance at Dunstan's face convinced her that this was not the time to inquire about the matter. Indeed, now that Gilcrest had disappeared into

NINA PYKARE

the throng, a deep frown furrowed Dunstan's forehead.

She looked out over the crowd in the direction of his glance and her heart lurched in her breast. She now knew the reason for that frown. Gilcrest had not disappeared. He stood some distance away by one of the booths and beside him, clinging to his arm in that wanton way of hers, stood the brazen creature from Almack's—Miss Castlemain, Dunstan had called her. Emily frowned. Even at this distance it was easy to see how her gown clung to her body.

Emily fought to control her feelings. Was Dunstan's anger caused by seeing that creature with Gilcrest? It certainly seemed so. All the good feelings she had been having about Dunstan and herself seemed suddenly foolish, the silly imaginings of a lovesick girl. Just because he treated her half decently and spoke to her as though she had some understanding—that didn't mean that he had any partiality for her. He was, after all, considerably older—more than thirty. Perhaps his feelings for her were more like those of a father for a daughter.

Emily swallowed over the sudden lump that formed in her throat. If that were so, she would never have the sons they had spoken of. For of one thing Emily was quite sure: She would never marry any man but Dunstan, no matter if she must become an old maid, the butt of every man's

206

joke. It would be Dunstan for her or no man.

She was trying to conquer the lump in her throat and blink back the tears that had suddenly appeared in her eyes when Bersford called out, "Look, there goes Sadler."

Emily looked up with the others. Slowly rising into the early evening sky was a great balloon. Beneath it hung a brilliantly painted car in which stood a young man waving several large cards. She could not read the messages on the cards, but she supposed they were instructions to his helpers on the ground.

They watched in silence as the balloon rose higher and higher. Emily noticed that Sarah was clutching Bersford's arm, and smiled. Love had changed Sarah from a competent companion to a skittish young woman fearful of the least thing that threatened her beloved.

Strange, thought Emily, stealing a glance at Dunstan, that love did not affect her like that. She had been quite serious in her earlier comments. She could not conceive of a situation in which Dunstan could not take ample care of himself.

As darkness slowly fell, the park took on an even more festive look as gay Chinese lanterns were lit. Emily occupied herself for some moments in gazing at the different designs painted on those nearest them. Some bore likenesses of Mr. Kean in his various characters. Some represented the

Great Mogul, the Tower of Babel, and even the Chinese pagoda on the bridge. Gazing at those to her right, Emily discovered the likeness of Alexander, Emperor of Russia, and quickly looked away. Thank God, he had gone back to Russia and his Russian and French women. At least he was no longer in London to spread false rumors about her.

She caught her breath as lanterns began to bloom on the Chinese pagoda on its bridge over the canal. The reflections of the lanterns sparkled in the water like a fairyland come true. She sighed, wishing she had the right to lean against Dunstan's shoulder as the so-proper Sarah was doing to Bersford at this very moment. A thought came to her. If they were walking about, then she could put her arm through his—for safety's sake, of course.

She turned to Dunstan. "Milord, do you suppose we might walk a little down by the canal? It looks so lovely there. Bersford and Sarah can keep our places."

She held her breath. Perhaps he would not like her idea.

But finally he smiled. "A capital suggestion. And after we return, if Bersford and Miss Parker wish to take a stroll, we may do the same for them."

The arrangements were soon made and Emily and Dunstan moved off across the grass, now sadly trampled by the feet of the multitudes. They had taken only a few steps when a great whooshing noise resounded through the air, causing Emily to clutch instinctively at Dunstan's arm.

"It's all right," he reassured her. "It's only the rockets going off. See?"

From above the pagoda and from various apertures in its sides rockets shot into the night air. A great variety of wheels and stars appeared on the pagoda and great flights of rockets whooshed higher, falling in slow showers of fire. Roman candles threw blue stars far up into the sky and great balls of fire went up to explode into innumerable sparks which seemed to fill the sky.

"Stay close to me," said Dunstan softly. "I do not like it that Gilcrest is about here somewhere."

"Yes, milord," answered Emily and clung even tighter to his arm.

As the fireworks continued to light up the sky, they moved on toward the canal. They were standing there, surrounded by others, watching the fireworks and the boats upon the canal, when suddenly there was a great roar and a stick from a rocket came crashing down among them, a stick six feet long.

Emily's arm was torn from Dunstan's and she was thrown roughly to one side as the crowd milled about in panic. "Dunstan!" she called, but in the confusion her bonnet was knocked down over her eyes and she felt herself in danger of falling under the trampling feet. With a feeling of great relief she felt a strong arm encircle her waist and half drag, half carry her out of the confusion. She might have known that Dunstan would take good care of her. He hurried her some distance from the crowd while she endeavored to straighten her bonnet so that she could see.

Finally, just as they stopped, she got the bonnet pushed up. A scream rose to her throat and died there. The man who had saved her from the crowd, whose hand now held hers so firmly in his own, was not Viscount Dunstan at all. Grinning at her cheerfully, stood Lord Gilcrest!

"Milord!" she exclaimed. "What are you doing?"

"I am saving you from destruction," he said smoothly. "Those rocket sticks are vicious things."

"Viscount Dunstan," she began, her eyes searching the crowd.

"He does not appear to be here," said Gilcrest suavely.

Emily tried to pull her hand free. "I must go. Please!"

But Gilcrest merely smiled. "Not so fast, my dear. I have waited a long time to get you alone. Now that Dunstan is out of the way I mean to press my suit."

His pressure on her fingers increased until she wanted to cry out in pain.

"Did Dunstan tell you that I made an offer for you?" he asked.

Emily shook her head. "No, no, he did not."

Gilcrest sighed heavily. "You see how difficult the man makes it for me. He forbids you to see me. He does not even inform you of my suit."

"Perhaps he knew that my answer would be no," said Emily, still struggling unsuccessfully to free her fingers.

Gilcrest smiled, but it was not a pleasant smile. "He has forced me to take this kind of step," he said. "A man should have a chance to speak his piece." He gave her hand a sharp tug and pulled her into his arms. She struggled to free herself, but it was quite useless. There seemed little sense in screaming, for the general level of the noise around them was so high that a scream would go completely unnoticed.

"I have conceived a mad passion for you," said Gilcrest. "I wish to make you my wife."

"I—I do not wish to marry," said Emily. "Please release me."

But Gilcrest shook his head. "Come, you are being unfair. I am not such a bad case. And once my passion has dissolved, as such passions always do, I shall give you leave to pursue your own adventures. I doubt that Alexander will return soon, but there are sufficient fish in the sea."

Emily stared at him in surprise. "You would give me leave to be—unfaithful?"

Gilcrest nodded. "Of course. And you will give me similar leave. Oh, we shall be quite happily matched." He smiled at her wickedly. "Besides, knowing of your affiliation with Alexander, I should hardly expect you to remain singleminded for long."

"Oh!" This picture so angered Emily that without thinking any further she used the strategy that Cousin Percy had once laughingly taught her long ago.

As he bent to cover her lips with his, she brought her knee up sharply into Gilcrest's groin. There was a strangled exclamation and his arms fell away from her. Emily gave him a great shove for good measure and sped away.

Fortunately the light of the lanterns made the park bright and she could see in what direction the benches lay. She could only hope that Dunstan had returned there and was not wandering aimlessly about in the crowd.

She jostled her way through the masses of people, never looking behind her. Several times rough hands clutched at her, but she hurried on. She would let nothing stop her. She must find Dunstan.

Finally she pushed her way through and could see Sarah, Bersford, and Dunstan huddled in a worried conference. She composed herself as best she could and hurried up to them.

Sarah saw her first. "Emily! Emily, my dear. Are you all right?"

"Yes, yes," Emily answered their queries with a smile. "When the rocket stick fell, I lost my grasp on his lordship's arm and was pushed to one side."

"The stick knocked me down," said Dunstan, putting one hand to his head. "Several people carried me to one side where I regained my senses."

"Oh! Are you all right now?" asked Emily.

The viscount nodded. "Yes. Aside from a small bump, I suffered no injuries. But please continue your story."

Emily felt the color flood her cheeks, but she determined to keep him from knowing about Gilcrest. He would be so angry, he might call the man out. And it was all unnecessary. No harm had been done.

"I was a little startled by being so rudely separated from you," she continued. "It took me a few minutes to get my bearings. Then, when I couldn't find you, I made my way here."

"It took you a long time," observed Dunstan. She could not tell if there was suspicion in his tone.

"The park is very crowded, and I was confused at first."

"And no one bothered you?" he asked gruffly.

Emily shook her head. There was little point in telling him about the clutching hands. He could do nothing about them now. "No," she lied. "No one bothered me. I'm just fine."

213

Dunstan continued to stare at her suspiciously but she forced herself to confront him boldly and finally he turned to Sarah. "I must admit that the accident has somewhat damped my enthusiasm for any more festivities. If you and Bersford do not mind, I believe I shall just take Emily home. I shall send the carriage back to fetch you later."

Sarah sprang to her feet. "No, no, milord. We shall come, too. I am myself quite fatigued."

"Yes," agreed Bersford. "We shall come with you."

The four of them began to make their way back toward the gate. The grounds of the park were so crowded that it was quite difficult to get through the people, but Dunstan and Bersford put their shoulders together and with determined effort cleared the way. Outside in the street the throng was even thicker and Emily clung to Dunstan's arm with both hands. Fear clutched at her heart. If she should get separated from him in this press of people . . . She refused to consider the subject any further. They would soon find the carriage and be safe.

"I'm afraid we shall have to walk for a space," Dunstan said. "I told the driver to wait several streets over. The crush will be less there."

Emily nodded and continued to cling to his arm. Eventually they made their way through the press into the area where there were relatively few people about.

Sarah heaved a sigh of relief and Emily echoed it. Glancing at Dunstan, she was surprised to see a thin trickle of blood on his cheek. "Milord! You are bleeding! You have been hurt badly."

He shrugged. "It's nothing. A small cut from the rocket stick. Parks will see to it shortly."

Still, she could not be convinced. She eyed him with concern until they reached the carriage and were all settled. Indeed, even on the drive home she kept glancing at him surreptitiously.

Finally he smiled at her. "Really, Emily, I assure you. It is nothing but a minor cut. Nothing to be concerned about, nothing at all."

"Yes, milord," she replied and resolutely kept her eyes to the fore from then on. If she were not careful, such oversolicitude would make him suspicious. Sarah, if she were not so deep in her feelings for Bersford, would probably have guessed her secret already. But now her companion's whole life was wrapped up in the plans for her coming wedding.

Dunstan had sharp eyes, however, and it would never do for him to think that his ward had formed a partiality for him. Anything of that nature should come first from him, must come first from him. It was love she wanted from him. Love—not pity.

## CHAPTER 15

The next morning found Emily restless and ill at ease. She very much disliked lying. It made her quite uncomfortable. But even having had more time to think about it did not change her decision. She felt quite sure that she had done the right thing. Gilcrest had not succeeded in his strategy and maybe now he was finally convinced that the decision to refuse to receive him was hers, not Dunstan's. She could only hope so. Certainly she wanted nothing to interfere with the rapport that had seemed to exist between herself and Dunstan. It was on that rapport, on that special feeling that had seemed to exist between them, that she rested her hopes for the future.

His lordship was out and she wandered into

the courtyard to contemplate the flowers. She felt anxious and considered working again in the flower beds, but good sense restrained her. She did not want his lordship to find her behaving childishly again.

She sank down on a bench and gave herself up to a reverie in which Dunstan had never become her guardian, in which that first look from across the room had been followed by another, and then another, all culminating in the viscount's offer for her hand in marriage. Emily sighed. There was nothing in this world that she wanted more than to be Dunstan's wedded wife. And nothing that was less likely to happen, commented a sad voice within her.

"Well, Coz," came a cheerful call and Emily looked up to see Cousin Percy. "Percy! Hello! What are you doing here?"

Though Uncle Cyril was his father and this house technically Percy's home, Emily was aware that he had his own rooms and seldom frequented this place.

"I have come to see you," he replied. "Does that seem so unusual?"

Emily did not know quite how to reply to this. It was rather odd for Percy to take the time for a friendly call. They had not been close for many years now, and in fact, he had not even bothered to show up at her coming-out ball.

218

"I have come to plead the cause of a friend," he explained cheerfully.

Emily nodded. That made more sense. "A friend of yours?"

Percy smiled. "Yes, a fine chap. Good looker. Handy at cards. Great man with the horses."

"What has this to do with me?" asked Emily in confusion.

"Why, the man wants to marry you." It seemed obvious to Percy.

Emily suppressed a smile. The attributes that he had felt indicated good husband material did not rate very high on her list. "And who is this paragon of virtue?" she asked with a grin. "Why doesn't he speak for himself?"

"He's tried," said Percy. But Dunstan has formed a dislike for him. Fine chap, Dunstan, but a little touchy about some things. He has taken a great dislike to my friend—some matter of a chit, I believe—so he will not allow him to bring his court to you."

Emily stared at Percy, her expression suddenly sober. "What is the name of this friend?" she asked suspiciously.

"Lord Gilcrest."

Emily felt a coldness spreading over her. "Gilcrest!"

Percy nodded. "Yes. He's really a capital chap, Emily. He's stood the brunt for me more than once, given me the ready out of his own pocket. You couldn't do better."

Emily stared at her cousin. "What do you know of Lord Gilcrest?" she asked finally.

Percy shrugged. "Like I told you, he's a fine chap."

"What about the cause of this quarrel between him and Dunstan? This—chit?"

Percy shrugged again. "The sister of one of Dunstan's old friends, Castlemain, I believe he was called. Got his in the war with old Boney. It seems Dunstan was after the chit and Gilcrest beat him to it. A simple matter. No cause to carry a grudge."

There was something to this story that didn't ring true. Emily could well imagine Gilcrest and Dunstan in competition over a woman. That kind of thing happened every day. What she could not imagine was any woman preferring Gilcrest. Certainly at Almack's Miss Castlemain had seemed very partial to Dunstan. Would she behave in that fashion if she cared for Gilcrest?

But perhaps there were other factors involved. Perhaps Gilcrest had deserted her, as men were so often fond of doing, and as he was certainly quite capable of. Or perhaps she had tired of him and so regretted her first choice and decided to pursue Dunstan after all.

"Emily," said Percy, tugging at her sleeve, "tell

ne, when can I arrange a meeting between you
nd Gilcrest?"

"Percy, you cannot. Such a thing is improper."

Percy grinned. "Come on, Emily. These things
re done every day in the week."

Emily frowned. "Perhaps by other women, but
ot by me. Besides, I do not like the man."

Percy looked crestfallen. "You haven't given
im a chance. You hardly know him."

Emily's frown deepened. "I know quite as much
f him as I wish to know. In fact, too much. No,
ercy, there is no use in your trying to prevail
pon me. I know your old tricks and no amount
f talk will convince me that I should regard Gil-
rest as a suitable alliance. Come now, tell me,
hat has he promised you? Or what do you owe
im?"

Percy was trying to compose himself and she
new with certainty that her guess had hit home.
This was not a matter of pure friendship for him.

"Oh, Emily, come on. Don't be after me like
hat. It's true I owe Gilcrest a little blunt. Bor-
owed a trifle the other night." He shuffled his
eet sheepishly. "But that has nothing to do with
his. Gilcrest is really a sound chap. I can't imag-
ne why you don't like him."

Emily shook her head. "Percy, think a little. A
nan who frequents White's every night? A ready
hand with the horses? Does that sound to you
ike a man designed for connubial bliss?"

Percy had the grace to look embarrassed. "Suppose not. Never thought of it that way. Just know he makes a good friend."

Even that Emily doubted. She sensed something in Gilcrest that disproved friendship. And what man would encourage his friend to gamble by loaning him more money? But she did not say any of this to Percy. It would make no sense to him.

"I'm sorry, Percy, truly I am. But Gilcrest is not the sort of man I would wish to marry."

Percy shrugged. "Well, I did the best I could. I'll just have to tell Gilcrest so."

Emily agreed. "That sounds like the wisest thing to do."

Percy nodded. "Well, since I failed to fulfill my mission, I guess I'd better just breeze along." He consulted his timepiece. "Time to get back to my favorite haunts. Got some friends waiting for me."

Emily tried to smile. Her heart was troubled by the kind of companions Percy was spending his time with, but she did not know how to caution him about them.

He was moving away from her when she suddenly rose and ran to hug him. "Percy, Percy, do be careful. Please!"

He held her off and looked at her in surprise. "Of course, I shall be careful. Whatever made you think I wouldn't?"

Emily swallowed over the lump in her throat.

222

"Nothing, nothing," she assured him. She gave him another hug, blinking back the tears that rose suddenly to her eyes. He was going into a dangerous world, a world where sharps abounded, where a man could be your friend and set you up for a pigeon at the same time. She buried her face in his shoulder for one more moment.

"Hello, Percy," came a deep voice from behind her. Startled, Emily sprang from Percy's arms and turned to see Dunstan regarding them coolly.

"Hello, Dunstan," said Percy, apparently not at all disconcerted by having been discovered in an embrace with his cousin. "Just stopped by to have a little chat with Emily here. We're childhood friends, you know. Used to get into the suds together."

"Indeed. I trust that you are no longer pulling her in after you." Dunstan's voice was completely polite—there was no hint of displeasure in it—but Emily was well aware that anger seethed below his calm surface. The telltale muscle in his jaw twitched uneasily. But even more than that was her awareness of the tension in the air. She did not see how Percy could not be aware of it, yet he seemed entirely at ease.

"No, I don't do that anymore," he replied with a rueful grin. "Though we did have our fun."

"Well," said Dunstan. "I should not want to interrupt your reminiscing of old times."

He made no move to leave them and, indeed,

continued to stare rather fixedly at Emily's cousin until he said, "Well, Emily, I'll be off now. Good-bye."

"Good-bye, Percy." She managed to get the words out, though her mouth had gone suddenly quite dry. She watched as he moved nonchalantly away, giving every appearance of aplomb.

He passed through the door into the house and Emily shifted her eyes to Dunstan, who was staring at her. Suddenly she found she could not bear to meet his eyes and turned to move toward the flowers.

"I am not impressed by Percy's act of innocence," said Dunstan sharply, causing her to whirl around to face him.

"I do not understand you, milord." Emily's voice betrayed her agitation.

"You understand me very well," said his lordship. "I knew your cousin Percy. He did not drop by just to pass the time of day with you."

His eyes probed deeply into hers as she confronted him. "It is pointless for you to try to hide this from me. You cannot hide anything from me."

"I was not trying to hide anything," cried Emily angrily. "You did not give me a chance to tell you anything. You immediately jumped to the conclusion that I was hiding something."

She felt compelled to explain her behavior. "I—I was hugging Percy because of—old times." She looked into his eyes for some evidence that he understood what she was talking about, but they were veiled and blank.

"I—I am concerned about Percy," she continued. "I fear he has fallen into bad company."

Dunstan raised a cynical eyebrow. "I collect that he has been in bad company for some time now."

Emily frowned. "Perhaps he has, but it only just came to me how vulnerable Percy is himself." She saw that he was regarding her closely and she floundered on. "I mean—before I was concerned about the—" She flushed. "About the young women that Percy might—might hurt. But now, now I see that Percy himself may be badly hurt."

"All this is very well," said the viscount. "But it does not give me an inkling as to the subject of your discussion."

"I am coming to that," said Emily. "Percy came to see me"—she sighed—"to see if I would—have a meeting—with—" She had to swallow several times before she could get the word out. "With Gilcrest."

"He what?" Dunstan's iron control broke and he stepped forward and grabbed her roughly by the shoulders.

"He wanted me to have a meeting with Gilcrest," she repeated, wincing from the pain where his grip had tightened.

"The stupid young pup! How dare he!" Dunstan was glaring at her so fiercely that she felt her knees begin to quake.

"Please, milord. Dunstan! You're hurting me." Tears of pain stood out in her eyes.

He loosed his grip slightly but the fierce frown on his face remained. "You will not receive Percy again, I'll see to that."

"Dunstan, you cannot forbid Percy his own father's house. Please, you have not allowed me to finish."

Still he did not release her arms. "Finish then."

"I told him I could not do such a thing, that Gilcrest was not a good man." A tear spilled over and rolled down her cheek, but she could not wipe it away. "He kept telling me that Gilcrest is his friend. It was then that I realized how vulnerable he is."

Dunstan stared at her for several moments. "There is more to this than you have told me."

She tried to keep from coloring, but in spite of herself the red flooded her cheeks.

"Come, Emily. Do not deny it. You do not lie well. Your face gives you away."

"He's—he's in debt to Gilcrest. It was for this reason that he could be prevailed upon to come see me."

Dunstan's face grew even darker. "How can you have concern for a man who would do such a vile thing? Certainly he knows that Gilcrest would not be good husband material."

Emily shook her head. "It was a bad thing to do, but Percy isn't bad. Selfish maybe, but not really bad."

Dunstan continued to frown. "You may make all the excuses you please for him, but I still see Percy as worse than irresponsible."

"I do not intend to see Lord Gilcrest," said Emily firmly. "Surely you know that I have refused to receive him. I told Percy that very plainly—also that I do not like the man. What more can you ask of me?"

"The truth," said his lordship bluntly. "Tell me the truth."

Emily's bewilderment was quite real. "I have told you the truth."

He shook his head and his eyes seemed to give off sparks. "You have not told me the truth."

"I told you everything Percy said."

"Of course you did. Do not look at me so innocently, Emily. Your statements about Gilcrest do not ring true," he said caustically.

Emily felt her anger rising again. "I abominate the man. Surely that should be abundantly clear to you by now."

"I thought it was." His jaw tightened and his lips settled into a thin firm line. "Until last night."

"Last night?" Emily felt the color flood her cheeks.

"As I told you, Emily, you are a very poor liar. Why didn't you tell me you met Gilcrest last night?"

"I didn't meet him." Her heart pounded in her throat. "I was separated from you when the rocket stick fell. My bonnet was pushed over my eyes. Someone grabbed me and hurried me away. I thought it was you."

She saw unbelief in his eyes. "I couldn't see. Everything was confusion. When he stopped and I got my bonnet up—only then did I know it was Gilcrest who had my hand. Please! You must believe me. I got away from him as soon as I could."

Dunstan's eyes held hers. "How could you do that? You did not escape my embrace."

"I—I know. But I did get away from Gilcrest. I wasn't gone long. You know that."

He nodded. "But I still do not see how you got away. Gilcrest is not a man to trifle with. Tell me how you accomplished it."

The scarlet flooded Emily's cheeks and her heart began to pound in her throat. "I—I cannot." She dropped her eyes momentarily.

"Of course you can. I am quite curious as to how you did it. Look me in the eye, Emily, and tell me how you did it."

She shook her head. "It's—it's too embarrassing."

"Then show me."

"Oh, no! I cannot!"

"Emily, I insist on knowing how you effected

228

your escape. As your guardian I command you to tell me."

She raised her eyes to his. "And you promise not to be angry with me?"

"Of course, I promise," he replied.

"It was something Percy taught me long ago." She paused to swallow. "A man's most—most vulnerable spot. I—used my knee—and—"

Dunstan's expression changed suddenly and he coughed, almost as though he were smothering a laugh. "That will be enough, Emily. I believe I get the gist of it. There's no need to go further. It appears that for once Cousin Percy taught you something worthwhile."

Emily nodded, taking heart from his acceptance. "It—it proved rather effective, milord."

Dunstan smiled dryly. "I'm sure it did." He coughed again discreetly. "I find that I must thank you for your solicitude toward me." His eyes twinkled at her and she was sure he was amused. "It was very generous of you not to demonstrate your trick on me, especially when I practically ordered you to."

Emily flushed again. "I—I would not want to hurt you."

For a long moment he stood looking into her eyes. She almost hoped that he was about to say the words she so longed to hear. But then he frowned again. "Please, Emily, you must believe me. Gilcrest is a dangerous man. He has ruined more than one young woman. I do not want him to add you to his list."

"He will not," said Emily firmly. "I assure you of that."

He did not completely believe her story yet; she saw that in his eyes. But the report of her trick had impressed him.

"I must leave you now, Emily. I have an appointment."

She nodded. "Yes, milord."

He seemed to grow suddenly aware that his hands were still on her shoulders and he let them fall away awkwardly. "I hope that I did not hurt you," he said apologetically.

"I am all right," replied Emily, hoping that there would be no bruises on her arms in the morning and resolving to cover them with long sleeves should there be.

"Good. Good-bye now."

He turned to go and suddenly she called out. "Dunstan, is there—nothing you can do to help Percy? No way to convince him?"

His lordship shook his head. "He's a pigeon ready for the plucking, Emily. He will simply have to learn for himself. He will not listen to me, you know that. In fact, if I should speak to him, it might only drive him further on, further into debt."

She nodded. "You're right, milord. But if you see any way to help him—"

"Then I will." He smiled at her briefly, then turned and strode away.

She watched him go, her heart beating in her throat, tears rising to her eyes as she considered how very much she loved him. Where was he going now? To Harriette Wilson or to the brazen Miss Castlemain? Oh, why, why, would he never come to her?

## CHAPTER 16

The days passed and Sarah's banns were called for the second time. Emily was quite pleased at her friend's happiness. Even her own prospects seemed a little brighter. If she could just avoid getting mixed up with Gilcrest or with Percy anymore, perhaps she could convince Dunstan that she was mature enough to deserve his regard.

She and Sarah spent many hours in grave consultation over the contents of Sarah's trousseau. They made two trips to the *modiste* before they could decide on the pattern for her wedding gown.

Other shopping trips filled up the days and Emily woke one morning to the realization that the wedding was little more than a week away.

Then she would lose her companion. She decided to seek out Dunstan. There was no point in waiting longer. They would have to find Sarah's replacement soon, for it would be highly improper for her to stay in the house with the viscount without some kind of chaperone.

She put on her green-sprigged muslin, brushed her curls, and went to find if his lordship was still about.

Fortunately he had not yet gone out and she found him in the library with a pot of tea. He looked up from a desk covered with papers. "Good morning, Emily."

"Good morning, milord."

What a pleasure it was to have him smile at her like that. "It has just struck me that we've very little time in which to find a replacement for Sarah."

He nodded. "I have just been considering that myself." He gave her a strange look. "Have you anyone in mind?"

Emily shook her head. "Not really. It will be impossible to find anyone as good as Sarah. Just so she's not too stuffy."

The viscount chuckled. "It would be most unkind—to both of you—to saddle you with such a companion." He paused. "I have someone in mind. A young woman—the sister of a friend of mine."

"What is she like?" asked Emily.

"She has been rather unfortunate in her choice

of companions," he said gravely. "But she has now regretted that. I believe your acquaintance would be beneficial to her."

Emily felt the color rising to her cheeks. It couldn't be possible. He couldn't mean to bring that terrible Miss Castlemain into the house! She stared at him. "Do I know this young woman?"

He shook his head. "No, you have not made her acquaintance, though you may have seen her on some occasion when we were out." He looked a trifle uncomfortable.

"Her name?" said Emily sweetly, keeping a tight rein on the anger seething within her.

"Miss Castlemain."

Emily bit her bottom lip to keep from screaming out at him. Finally she felt calm enough to reply. "You quite surprise me, milord. You are so extremely solicitous about my reputation, yet you propose for me a companion of the poorest quality. Gilcrest's rejected plaything. How will it look to the *ton*, do you think, if the creature that has been hanging all over Dunstan comes suddenly to live in the same house with him? Tell me, milord, who will serve as chaperone for Miss Castlemain, whose admiration for you is quite as evident as her damped petticoats?"

He rose from the desk and came toward her, his eyebrows drawing together fiercely. "This sarcasm is unbecoming to you," he said curtly. "Barbara

Castlemain is a young woman in need of assistance. For the sake of her brother, whose memory I revere, I intend to do all I can to help her. I am attempting to save her from destruction. It would seem to me that you, who have certainly made your share of mistakes, would be a little more compassionate to a fellow creature."

By now Emily's anger had complete control of her. True, his words stung somewhat, but it was not lack of compassion that made her rage so, it was pure jealousy. "You do not fool me, milord Dunstan. I have seen this young woman hanging on your arm. And now you want to bring her into the house where you will have easy access to her. Well, I refuse to be your accomplice in this!" Her breath was coming fast and quick and she glared at him.

"You are behaving foolishly," said Dunstan. "My concern for Barbara Castlemain is purely altruistic. I have no desire for her. In fact, I am enamored of a young woman and I expect to marry as soon as I get your affairs in order."

Emily felt her knees buckle. He was going to marry!

"But, but . . . You never said."

He eyed her coldly. "As I have told you on several occasions, I am the guardian here. I have loved this young lady for some time now. Now, if you'll excuse me, since you refuse refuge to a fellow creature in distress, I must make other arrangements for her future." With that he strode off, leaving her in stunned shock.

She sank into a nearby chair. He was going to marry! All her dreams came crashing down around her. She had never even had a chance. She blinked back the tears and swallowed hastily. How fortunate that he had never discovered her partiality for him. She could not bear to have him pity her. That would be even worse than his contempt.

She sat there for some minutes, trying to rally her numbed senses. She shivered. She could not bring herself to have another man. And to keep Dunstan any longer from the woman he loved was unfair. Nor could she imagine living on in the house with him and his bride. Such a future held too much agony.

She could no longer stay in London—that much seemed clear. After Sarah's wedding she would return to Essex, perhaps find a comfortable middle-aged woman as companion. There she would settle into the life of a spinster.

She was still sitting, trying to make herself realize that all hope was gone, when Sarah finally found her. "Emily! What are you doing in here? Don't you remember, we're going shopping?"

Emily shook her head and pressed trembling hands to her temples. "I can't, Sarah, I just can't. I've got a headache so bad I can't think."

Sarah's plain face reflected concern. "Oh, dear,

then I shan't go either. I can't leave you like this."

"Please, Sarah, take Rose and go," Emily pleaded. "I need only to lie upon my bed for a while in quiet. Then I shall be fine."

Sarah still did not seem convinced. "Come, Sarah," Emily coaxed. "You can do nothing for me by remaining here. I shall feel infinitely worse if I keep you from your pleasures."

Sarah considered this. "Well, if you're quite sure."

"I am, Sarah. I am. Come, you shall see me safely lying in the dark and then you can be upon your way. I insist on it."

They made their way up the stairs and Emily removed her shoes and lay upon the bed. Sarah fussed around, making sure that everything was right and then, with a little frown, left for her shopping.

Lying there in the darkness of the curtained bed, Emily let the tears come. It seemed incomprehensible that Dunstan should love another woman. These last weeks the feelings between them had been better and better. She was quite sure of that. How could she have not sensed this in him?

Tears rolled down her cheeks and sobs shook her body. Young women no longer died of broken hearts, she thought numbly. She must learn to live with this. There was nothing else to do.

She had finally drifted off into an exhausted

sleep when she was wakened by a brisk tap on the door. "An urgent message, miss," said Jeffers when she went to open it.

The message was in an unknown hand and Emily's fingers trembled as she tore it open. Her first thought was that something dreadful had happened to Dunstan.

Quickly her eyes scanned the message. It was not Dunstan, it was Sarah! A rearing horse had kicked her and she could not be moved. Emily muttered the address aloud as she grabbed up bonnet, shawl, and reticule. She must find a hack. She must get to Sarah immediately!

The note fell from her fingers as she sped down the stairs, past the startled Parks and out into the street.

Now, which way was the nearest hack stand? Emily hurried off down the street. Dear God! Sarah injured—and so badly she couldn't be moved! Belatedly Emily thought of Bersford, but she had no idea how to reach him. First she must get to Sarah. Half running, half walking, she hurried down the street.

There was a terrible stitch in her side and her breath was coming in gasps when she heard the sound of a carriage pulling up beside her. A cheerful voice called out, "Miss Penthorne. Halloo! What are you doing roving about the streets like this?"

Emily looked up to find Gilcrest eyeing her with concern.

"It's Sarah," she gasped. "She's hurt. I—I am on my way to her."

"Of course, of course." Gilcrest was all solicitude. "Here, get in. We will go there instantly."

Somewhere in the back of Emily's mind alarm bells rang. She knew that it was indiscreet to be seen riding with Gilcrest. But Dunstan was already lost to her and she had to get to Sarah before it was too late. In her anxiety, she forgot about everything but her friend.

"Oh, thank you," she cried, accepting his help up. "I am so worried about her."

"The direction," said Gilcrest soothingly. "I must give the driver the direction."

"Of course." Emily rattled it off. "It is not a street I am familiar with," she said nervously. "I cannot imagine what she was doing there."

Gilcrest passed the direction to the driver and leaned back in the seat beside her. "Compose yourself, Miss Penthorne. We will get there as quickly as possible."

As the carriage moved off at a good clip, Emily relaxed just a little. Soon she would be by Sarah's side. "When you have left me with Sarah," she said. "I should like you to do me another favor."

"Of course, dear lady. Whatever you wish."

"Sarah's betrothed, Bersford. If you can find him and send him to her."

240

Gilcrest nodded. "Of course. With the greatest speed."

His hand covered hers briefly and she did not pull away. After all, he was being quite kind. "Come, my dear, you really must compose yourself. Your friend will be all right."

"But she has been kicked by a horse," cried Emily. "Such accidents can be fatal."

Gilcrest made no reply to this, but Emily was gratified to find that he urged the driver to go faster. It did seem a little odd to her that they should be traveling the back streets, but then there was less traffic on them and the carriage could go faster.

She closed her eyes in order to ask the Almighty for help for Sarah. Surely if anyone deserved his help, it was Sarah, who after so many years of unhappiness and waiting, was finally to come into her own. She must not die now, Emily thought. She must not.

When she opened her eyes again, Emily was surprised to see that they were passing into the country. "Surely Sarah could not have come this far!"

Gilcrest gave her a peculiar smile. "I am only following the directions you gave me."

Emily shook her head. "There must be some mistake. Sarah could not have come this far. Please, take me back. I must find her."

Gilcrest continued to smile oddly. "We are not going back to the city."

Cold fear struck at Emily's heart. "I must find Sarah," she cried. "She's been hurt!"

Gilcrest shook his head. "Your friend, Miss Parker, was in excellent health when last I saw her—shopping on Bond Street."

"I do not understand." Emily knew that her hands were trembling and she fought to control them.

"It is very simple really." Gilcrest adjusted his gloves. "You have refused to receive me, but I do not give up easily." His look sent a cold shiver of fear over her. "So I have been watching your activities. I knew that sooner or later my chance would come."

Emily listened, her heart in her throat. He was saying that Sarah was not hurt, that this was some plot of his! A new fear washed over her.

She looked toward the side of the carriage. Even though it was going at quite a speed, perhaps she could throw herself out. Almost as though he divined her intent, Gilcrest's hand closed around her wrist with an iron grip. "You are not going anywhere, my dear. At least, not anywhere outside this carriage."

"You must let me go," cried Emily. "Take me back this instant!" She tried to free her wrist, but was unsuccessful.

Gilcrest smiled again, a smile that chilled her blood. "We will come back to London eventually," he said as the carriage clattered through the trees. But when you return, it shall be as my wife."

Emily stared at him. "This is impossible. Do you think I would marry you after this awful thing you have done to me?"

Gilcrest shrugged. "It was a simple thing. I just waited till I saw Miss Parker out alone and surmising, correctly, that you must be at home, dispatched the note and you fell nicely into my hand."

"You cannot force me to marry you."

Gilcrest raised an eyebrow. "Perhaps not, but by the time we get to Scotland, you may have changed your mind. The journey is rather long and the nights are cold. You will belong to me, in fact if not in law, long before we reach the parson."

"No." Emily spat the word at him. "I will never be your wife. Never! Never!"

His grip on her wrist tightened cruelly. "You'll sing quite another song before long. Your good name will be completely ruined. No decent man will have you."

Emily shuddered. Dunstan! What would he do?

"You will be sorry if you try to wed me," she said icily. "Or take unlawful liberties. I have a guardian."

243

Gilcrest laughed loudly. "Yes, I know. The inestimable Dunstan. He kept me from having Barbara Castlemain. Just as the little bird was about to fly into my net, he stopped her. But this time I will win." His face lit up in a way that sickened her. "What pleasure I shall find in seeing his face when you return—despoiled."

Emily felt waves of fear washing over her. She must strive to keep her head. She could not give in to panic. Think! She must think. She had rushed out of the house in such a hurry that no one would have any inkling of her destination. When Dunstan returned and found her gone, what would he do? What would he think?

Could she change Gilcrest's mind? The man was obviously not thinking clearly. He had failed to consider the repercussions of this deed. That there would be repercussions Emily was quite sure.

She looked around her again. There must be something she could do, some way to escape him. He would have to stop the carriage sometime. He could not hold her wrist all the way to Scotland. She would keep herself in readiness for any eventuality. In the meantime she would try talking to him.

"Lord Gilcrest?"

"Yes, my dear." His eyes gloated over her in a way that made her flesh crawl.

"Have you considered this carefully?" she asked.

"Have you given any thought to what will happen to you when Dunstan discovers this?"

Gilcrest laughed again. "Dunstan already suspects your virtue," he said. "No matter your protestations to the contrary, you will be legally mine. There is nothing he can do then."

"He can call you out."

"Yes, so he can. But dueling is illegal these days and somehow the news would leak out so that the duel would be stopped. Dunstan would be in trouble, not I."

Emily let this sink in. It appeared that Gilcrest had considered everything. She shuddered at the thought of the fate awaiting her, but she would not give in easily. "I shall never consent to marry you," she repeated firmly. "Never."

Gilcrest shrugged. "Certain young women have begged me on their knees for that favor," he observed dryly. "You may well join them."

"I will never do that," declared Emily hotly.

"We shall see. A woman with a tarnished reputation has little chance in the marriage mart. No one will have you if you come back from such a trip with me."

"I—I should rather become an incognita than be your wife!" she cried.

Gilcrest laughed harshly. "What a rich ending that should be to Dunstan's attempts to preserve you pure. Unfortunately I cannot indulge myself in such speculations. I much prefer our marriage, for other reasons. He kept me from the Castle-main, but this time I will win."

This was the second time he had mentioned Barbara Castlemain, Emily realized. "How did he do that? How did he keep her from you?" she asked. Here was her chance to learn something. And, perhaps while she was doing so, she could conquer the fear that was rising to choke her.

Gilcrest frowned. "The girl was ripe. She heeded all my advice, dressed as I wished. I had persuaded her to meet me alone. Dunstan got wind of it and talked her out of it. She has ignored me since."

Emily felt a prick of conscience. She had mis-judged Dunstan in regard to Castlemain's sister. She could see that now. He had only been acting to protect an innocent girl.

"You should have agreed to meet me when I sent Percy as my envoy," Gilcrest continued. "That would have saved me a great deal of trouble and spared you some pain. Now I have spent con-siderable time in running you down and therefore my sport may be justifiably more cruel."

Waves of weakness swept over Emily. Whatever Gilcrest intended for her, it would not be pleasant. This was more than an abduction by an enterpris-ing fortune hunter. This was a plot of revenge against Dunstan, and to the end of accomplishing that revenge, Gilcrest would spare no one.

He glanced up at the sky that was beginning to darken. "Whip up the horses," he called to the driver. "I am anxious to reach the inn."

As the carriage careened along the winding road, Emily tried to collect her senses. When they reached the inn, she would do what she could: throw herself upon the mercy of the landlord, or perhaps some of the guests. Surely someone would listen to her. But reason told her that the people at the inn would care little for her and surely Gilcrest had some convincing story already prepared —a runaway wife or some such thing.

His hand still held her wrist, and as the carriage jostled over the rough road, she considered rising and struggling with him. If they both fell from the carriage, perhaps his grip on her would loosen. She might be able to run off and hide in the darkness.

She sat quietly, gathering her strength, waiting for the right moment to take him unawares. But then, just as she was about to move, he yanked her violently toward him. "I am tired of waiting," he said as his arms encircled her trembling body. "I shall have a kiss now."

Emily fought with all her strength to prevent his lips from reaching hers. As she panted and struggled in his arms, she heard very vaguely the sound of pounding hooves. It put no hope in her heart. Anyone passing by would only believe that a lord and his inamorata were resolving a little difference of opinion.

Suddenly the carriage came to such an abrupt halt that Emily was thrown to the floor. Her first thought, when she regained her breath, was escape. Then she heard the sounds of struggle and a muttered oath.

Elation flooded her body! That voice! It had to . . . It was—Dunstan!

She pulled herself up onto the seat of the carriage and saw that Dunstan and Gilcrest were fighting fist to fist, while off to one side stood Bersford, one hand gripping the collar of the driver.

Dear God! They had found her. Emily's eyes filled with tears. How they had done it she could not begin to say, but she offered up a prayer of gratitude for her deliverance.

Then the terrible thought struck her. To be sure, Dunstan had saved her, but he would never know that she had not come willingly. Gilcrest was sure to stick to the story of the elopement. And how could she expect Dunstan to believe her? All the circumstances pointed to her willingness to go with Gilcrest. Her alleged headache, the receipt of the note, her precipitate exit—all this conspired to prove her guilty. And she no longer had the note—the only piece of evidence that Dunstan might believe. Somewhere in her mad rush to reach Sarah she had lost it.

Tears flowed down her cheeks. No matter what she said, he would not believe her.

Finally Dunstan delivered a powerful uppercut to Gilcrest's chin that stretched the man lifeless on the ground. Turning, the viscount faced the carriage.

It was growing dusk, but there was more than sufficient light to show Emily the anger on his face. Grimly he reached up into the carriage and dragged her out. "Little fool! How many times did I tell you to be careful?" His chest rose and fell with the exertion of his battle.

Emily could not stop the tears that ran down her face. "It was not my fault," she cried. "Truly it wasn't."

He shook her roughly. "Oh, no?" Then he glared at her. "I talked to you and talked to you. I thought you had a modicum of common sense. But no, you must behave like a ninny and go running off half-cocked over such a Banbury tale."

Relief made Emily's knees weak. "You know!" she stammered. "You know he tricked me!"

He nodded. "Thanks to Jeffers who picked up the note when you dropped it. And Sarah who arrived home some half an hour after your departure."

Now that she was safe, Emily began to tremble violently. "How did you know what road to take?"

He smiled grimly. "This is the best road to Scotland. I thought Gilcrest wanted your inheritance, so it stood to reason he would try to force you into marriage. He went the direct route because he did not think his trick would be discovered so soon."

Emily shuddered. "He's—he's a horrible man. I was so afraid."

"You should have been," agreed Dunstan curtly. "You should never have gotten into his carriage like that. That was sheer stupidity."

Emily looked into the eyes so close to her own. "I know," she said quietly. "I'm sorry."

He stared at her in amazement. "No more excuses, no more defenses?"

Emily shook her head. "No more, milord. I have behaved very badly and caused you a great deal of trouble." For the first time she noticed the great bruise on his cheek and without thinking her fingers went out to touch it gently. "I am sorry. I think it best that I go back to Essex now." She swallowed painfully. "You have your own life to live."

"I cannot leave you exposed to the machinations of fortune hunters like him." He indicated the fallen Gilcrest.

"I do not intend to marry," Emily began, but Dunstan interrupted her.

"That solves no problem. As long as you are available, the men will be after your inheritance."

Bersford chuckled. "I can see only one solution to this dilemma," he observed ruefully. "If you wish to keep the young lady safe, you must marry her yourself."

Emily gasped. "Bersford! You can't mean it!"

Her eyes met Dunstan's and she was surprised to see him smiling. "Capital idea, Bersford. The very answer to our problem."

"You are mad—both of you," cried a distraught Emily. "You, Bersford to propose marriage for such a reason." She turned accusing eyes on Dunstan. "And you! Did you not just tell me that you are enamored of a young woman? What of her feelings in the matter?"

Dunstan grinned roguishly. "I am confident that if you agree to marry me, she will have no objections."

Emily's head was spinning. "But love, what of love?"

Dunstan's eyes looked deep into hers and again they seemed to hold a question. "What of love, Emily? Could you love me?"

The color flooded her cheeks. "Milord! Your question is unseemly—and irrelevant. You love another lady. Why don't you declare your love to her?"

"I am attempting to do so," he replied dryly. "But she seems determined not to hear me."

"I do not understand," replied Emily.

Dunstan pulled her closer. "Let me tell you a little story. Last winter on a short leave I attended a ball given by Lady Cholmondoley."

Emily's heart raced in her breast.

"While there I looked across the room and caught the eye of a most beautiful young woman. I did not seek her out for several reasons. First, she was very young, and second, I had to return immediately to the front. But this spring, the war over, I hurried to London to discover the young lady and offer her my hand in marriage. Imagine my surprise—and chagrin—at seeing her stand beside the road quizzing me and at discovering that I was to be her guardian."

"But I only stared so long because it was you," cried Emily. "And I had dreamed of you all winter."

"I could not press my intention without first giving other suitors a chance, especially when it appeared that you detested me. And you drove me near to distraction with your behavior with Alexander—and Gilcrest. But lately, when you turned down all offers, I began to have hope that my feelings for you were reciprocated."

"Oh!" cried Emily, happily throwing herself into his arms. "They are! They are! I have loved you all these months. And how I have envied Harriette Wilson and that Castlemain."

Dunstan stared at her in amazement. "Little Harry? Why, I haven't been to her establishment for five or six years. And as for Barbara Castlemain, I told you the truth. Her brother was my dearest friend and at his death I felt responsible for her."

Emily hung her head. "I am sorry for the things I said about her. You were right to reprimand me."

"There was a certain degree of wisdom in your anger," he said. "It would be rather foolish to have her in the house, considering her partiality for me. I have found her a place in a good home where she will be safe from men like Gilcrest."

"I am glad for that," replied Emily.

For a long moment they stood, looking fondly into each other's eyes.

"For heaven's sake, man," cried Bersford. "Kiss the girl and let's get back to London. By this time Sarah will be in a terrible stew."

With a smile Emily raised her face to the viscount and eagerly he complied. It had really happened, thought the shaken Emily, as he released her. He really did love her!

Leaving his driver to care for the now-moaning Gilcrest, Dunstan swung up into the saddle and helped Emily up behind him. "I trust it will not inconvenience you to ride this way," he said cheerfully. "Since we shall call the banns at our first opportunity, I do not think it will harm your reputation. Do you agree?"

"Oh, yes, milord," cried Emily, clasping him

joyfully from behind. "Only let us hurry back to tell Sarah the wonderful, wonderful news."

With that they rode off toward London and a future of love together.

## Love—the way you want it!

# *Candlelight Romances*